Coldarius The Origin of Gallium Book 1

D.L. Hannah

Contents

Isis, this is our second series! How about that?

Chapter 1

Gallium awakened to the sun's energizing rays beaming down on his face. The smell of bacon and cooked apples wafted into his bed chamber. He pictured his MotherForm in the dining chamber, preparing the morning meal for the family.

The sound of an ax splitting wood meshed with happy ChildForms playing beneath his window. Today was the day of his nineteenth summer. Although his family couldn't afford the grand LifeCelebrations the royal families were accustomed to, his ParentForms had worked hard to make each day of life special for all of their ChildForms.

He was the youngest of seven and the second MaleForm. His brother was over a decade older than him and had just finished his doctoral studies. His mother, who had obtained her teaching credentials before she married their father, was proud to have a physician in the family.

Their sisters had married and left the family home years ago to venture out on their own. Having no intended, he had no plans to marry anytime soon. He closed his eyes and settled into the firmness of the mattress.

Fantasies of marrying Princess Dellah, the most beautiful WomanForm in Coldarius, drifted across his mind. Unlike the rigid caste system of Platirius, it wasn't rare for Coldarian commoners to marry above their class. Still, he knew it would never be. She was engaged to King Dubian.

His parents weren't surprised when he'd chosen to study horticulture. He'd loved growing things since he was a young ChildForm. Amos and Etienne Barrios firmly believed in making sacrifices so their sons would be educated.

They couldn't have been happier when he graduated at the head of his class. Now he'd been selected by Princess Dellah to design and cultivate gardens in a new wing of King Carlomon's palace.

It was the grandest of opportunities—to be employed by the royal family commanded a lot of respect. They were happy none of their ChildForms would struggle in life.

Etienne set aside a pan and approached the bottom of the staircase. "Gallium, are you awake? You don't want to be late to meet with Princess Dellah."

She knew he wouldn't be late, but reminding him made her feel needed. Now that he would be leaving home to live at the palace, loneliness had slowly crept up on her, leaving her struggling to find things to occupy her time.

"I'm coming," he said, throwing back the covers. "I'm getting ready now."

He entered the bath chamber to bathe and shave. His family wasn't wealthy, nor were they poor. Their home, designed by Amos, was the most coveted in the neighborhood.

Having no formal education, he made a comfortable living designing homes and various buildings in Coldarius. He was the first to call if you wanted a job done right. He sniffed the air with pleasure as she served up the fragrant beef sausages, eggs, and apple fritters they'd have for breakfast.

"Is he all right?" he asked. "He's not getting nervous, is he?"

"Now, when have you ever known our Gallium to be nervous?" she asked, never taking her eyes off transferring the hot sausage rounds to the serving plate.

He looked toward the spiral stairway before sitting at the table. "You're right. It was a silly question."

She set the platter in front of him and turned to grab the bowl of eggs. "Silly questions don't exist. Only the most curious minds receive satisfaction."

He reached for a linen cloth. Spreading it across his lap, he said, "I had a chance to see where he'll live. I didn't go farther than the fence, but the grounds are very well-kept. He'll have a small cottage and won't have to share a room with anyone."

She smiled and sat down next to him. "Princess Dellah must be pretty impressed with our son to grant him permission to live on his own."

Nearly everyone hired to work for King Carlomon shared living quarters a short distance from the palace, but Gallium would be living on the palace grounds. That was a first for a

Coldarian born outside of the king's family. The royals were impressed with his natural acumen for growing things.

His fruit, vegetables, and flowers were the biggest and sweetest anyone had ever seen. He also knew how to change the structure of plants—transforming them into powders and serums. Some were used as medicine and remedies in the medical chamber. Others were used for chemical weapons.

He suspected that was the reason King Carlomon wanted him to be close—his son's unique ability to make weapons for warfare. No one in Coldarius was skilled enough to emulate him. Growing gardens for his daughter was a plus. Yet, a kingdom without strong defensive tactics was vulnerable.

While he was proud Gallium's abilities were essential to the royal family, he didn't know how to feel about the substances he created. Some would drive Beings to madness or worse—to execute themselves or others. He'd reared him to be a bright young MaleForm with a kind and gentle spirit. He didn't want that to change.

"Stop worrying about him," Etienne admonished. "He's not a young ChildForm anymore. He knows what he's doing."

Amos looked up at her in surprise, then smiled. She'd been able to hone in on his feelings since their first date. "I'm aware, Wife. I just..."

She adjusted his sweater. "He'll be fine. He's going to work for King Carlomon—the finest ruler Coldarius could ask for. He's been very good to all of us." A dark shadow fell over her pretty features. "Now, had that awful King Dubian wanted him, I would've forbidden him to go."

He reached for more sausages. "Now, Etienne, we don't know the whole story!"

She flicked her napkin at him. "Don't know the whole story? Are you sure about that? Old King Anemi was so evil, not even the devil could finish him off. Then all of a sudden, he's dead. Now that's not the worst part."

She leaned in closer to him. "Two months later, Prince Dimaro died under mysterious circumstances too. You don't find that suspicious? What are the chances two royal MaleForms of the same bloodline expire in such a short span of time?"

He forked up a batch of the steaming eggs. "You should've applied for the justice council instead of teaching. Your penchant for uncovering imaginary crimes is legendary."

She swatted his thigh.

"Ouch," he said, spilling his PotterBerry tea. Grabbing another napkin, she soaked up the tea before it spilled onto the floor.

He smiled at her as she refilled his cup. "Admit it. You're a born detective."

"Tease if you must, but even you can't ignore that all the signs point to King Dubian being a murderer!"

He took another sip of the hot tea. "Darling, listening to gossip isn't going to solve anything."

She bit into the flaky fritter. "I'm listening to my brain—not gossip. That MaleForm has been evil since before he could walk.

He's just like his father! Poor Caraleigh. She was foolish enough to fall for his lies."

"I don't feel sorry for her," he muttered.

Her mouth dropped. "Amos!"

His mustache twitched. "Well, I don't. What WomanForm knowingly copulates with a married MaleForm? She was as dense as those copper pots Gallium grows things in. She actually believed King Anemi would've left Queen Zherta for her. What utter nonsense!"

She took a bite of sausage and chewed. "Oh, she was young. She didn't know any better! The poor thing died giving birth to King Dubian. His father was so cruel, he never told him about her until he was much older. He didn't show her an ounce of sympathy—he painted her as a whore in front of his own son!"

He placed another fritter on her plate. "Queen Zherta stepped in to be his MotherForm. That should've been enough."

She stared at him. "You aren't serious? She was worse than her husband. She only wanted to take him in so others would praise her. I heard she had him beaten for the slightest mistakes. Repeatedly."

Slathering a generous amount of butter on her fritter, she said, "If you ask me, they should've let him be shipped off to another planet. Many families are unable to have ChildForms. He would've had a better life than what he had with those cold-blooded monsters."

"What are you two talking about?" asked Gallium.

"Nothing," she said, uncovering the serving dishes.

She spooned generous portions of food on his plate and set it before him. Amos filled his cup with a hot drink made from one of his new hybrid plants—CocoBerry. It tasted like strawberries and chocolate. When hot cream was stirred into the steeped CocoBerries, it was divine.

"Thank you," he said. "You could've waited for me before you started eating."

She patted his shoulder. "You lose track of time when you get to styling that luxurious hair of yours. The food would've been colder than King Anemi's heart before you appeared."

Gallium laughed. "Ah! So that's what you were talking about—the Platirians! Do you still think King Dubian is a killer?"

Amos rolled his eyes toward the Heavens. "Please don't get her started," he begged.

She pointed at Amos. "Go on and make fun. But you mark my words—no good will come of Princess Dellah marrying him. She'll regret it as sure as I'm sitting here!"

"Well, it's her choice," said Amos. "Maybe she'll change her mind."

"She was promised to Prince Dimaro, not King Dubian. I think she's only marrying him because of the merger."

Amos eyed Gallium, who was listening intently. "Let's not discuss this in front of Gallium? I don't want him involved in anything about King Dubian."

She nodded firmly. "On that? We agree. Let's let it rest. What's done is done."

Gallium looked from his mother to his father. "Hey, I'm not a ChildForm, you know? I won't fall apart hearing King Dubian is a total psycho."

Her fork stopped midway to her mouth. "A total psycho? What language is this you're speaking? Have you been watching those dreadful Humans on the TranScreen again? I don't want you speaking as they do. They're idiots!"

He laughed. "True, but I think some of their language is useful."

She looked doubtful. "There's nothing 'useful' about Humans. They wouldn't hesitate to kill you if you were on their planet. Don't go getting any ideas about making friends with them if our king sends you on missions."

"I won't. But I think going to Earth would be exciting! Learning their languages would make passing as one of them easier."

Dr. Ezra Barrios had been sent on numerous assignments to Earth. His latest quest was in a place called Nazi Germany in 1934. Gallium thought the horrors he described were awful.

Human males, females, and children were persecuted by a Human male they called Adolf Hitler. His mission was to observe them and report back to the king. Researching Human interaction was vital to King Carlomon's plans.

While King Anemi supported Human experimentation on Platirius, it was prohibited on Coldarius. King Carlomon wanted to expand Coldarius's borders to make room for Humans who sought asylum away from Earth. However, this couldn't be done until a merger between Coldarius and Platirius was finalized.

Unlike the other galactic kings, King Carlomon was open to peaceful negotiations with the Humans. He and Princess Dellah, who held a seat on Coldarius's justice council, were sympathetic to their suffering.

Before she died, it had been Queen Elia's dream to share Coldarius with other Beings who were unhappy living on their home planets. It was important to her grieving husband to grant her final wish. But not all Coldarians agreed with his plans. Humans were despised and mistrusted on every planet outside of Earth.

Galactic Beings saw the greed and hatred that flowed among them. They saw no reason to allow them entry into their planets. Many kings publicly sympathized with King Carlomon, but he was a laughingstock in private.

King Anemi secretly hated his kind-hearted nature. In his eyes, such a weak-minded king had no business leading an empire. He was open to merging with Coldarius for a single reason—greed. Coldarius's lands were rich in sapphire, topaz, and other precious jewels Platirius couldn't produce alone.

Being the leader in manufacturing platinum and diamonds wasn't enough. He wanted Platirius to be the wealthiest planet in the galaxy. A union with Coldarius would make it a reality.

"What do you think of the merger between us and Platirius?" asked Gallium. "Do you think it's a good idea?"

Etienne scooped up a mound of eggs. "We're not discussing Platirius at this table."

Amused, he shook his head. "I'm in my nineteenth summer. When will you stop treating me like I'm still in primary school?"

She winked at Amos. "When you get married," she said. "That's when we'll include you in our conversations."

Gallium sighed and cut into his sausages. They spent the rest of their time carefully avoiding the subject of King Dubian and Princess Dellah. He finished and rose to place his plate in the sanitizer.

She watched sadly as he washed his hands and stretched. It would be his last breakfast at home. Sensing the quick shift in her mood, he turned to embrace her, lifting her several inches off the floor.

She ducked her head into his shoulder. "When did my little son become so big and strong?"

Hearing her voice crack, he sought to find the right words to comfort her. "You'll hardly miss me. I'll be back to bother you and Father so much you'll chase me back to the palace."

She smoothed back his hair. "I'm going to hold you to that. Make sure you don't forgo mealtimes, and don't work yourself to the point of illness."

He stiffened, then relaxed as he set her down. His parents didn't know his secret, and he wasn't sure he was ready to reveal it to them...or anyone. How could he explain what he'd discovered when even he didn't understand it?

"There goes another lecture," he teased. "Guess it's time to go."

He smiled down at her while trying to ignore the tears in her eyes. He hated seeing her cry.

His father nodded. "I'll walk with you. I need to collect the payment for the new dining chamber I built for the military."

He, too, wanted to spare her from seeing their son off. Out of all her ChildForms, she had the strongest bond with him. She'd almost lost him in childbirth.

For the first two years of his life, he'd been so weak that no one thought he'd survive. But he'd beaten the odds. Now he stood before her healthy and strong, ready to face whatever life brought his way. She couldn't have been prouder of him.

G eneral Iham met them in the middle of the square. "Amos! Are you on your way to the palace?"

He smiled at his old friend. "Of course, General! You know the happiest days in my lifespan are collection days!"

Giving him a good-natured slap on the shoulder, General Iham said, "The dining chamber you built is state of the art! King Carlomon raved over how you connected it to the bunkers and bed chambers. Now we don't have to go off-site to eat anymore. I knew you were the best one for the job!"

"I can't thank you enough for referring me. It was an honor to perform the service for His Majesty's army. If we're going to fight off our enemies, we need you to live in comfort."

"I think your day is just about to get better." He held up his hand. On his palm, a series of numbers appeared.

Amos blinked twice. "You've already transferred the funds! But wait, that's more than what I contracted the job for!"

He nodded happily. "Oh yes. Much more! King Carlomon was so impressed with your work, he added a large bonus. Don't go saying it's too much! On top of building the finest dining chamber we've ever had, you finished construction ahead of schedule. You deserve every bit of it."

Amos and Gallium looked at each other, rendered speechless by the unexpected good fortune.

"You know, I don't think I've ever seen a day where you couldn't speak. Maybe this will move your tongue, eh? The king sent me to find you. He's requested for you to be his new chief contractor."

He held up his palm again. A new sum of funds appeared under the first deposit. "Once you accept his offer, you'll be commissioned to build for him permanently. He only wants you, Amos. I don't think I have to tell you what an amazing opportunity this is."

He didn't. His head was spinning. It was already an honor for Gallium to be hired at the palace. Now Amos would be joining him. He thought of Etienne. Would they have to live apart?

General Iham answered the unspoken question. "The offer extends to your entire family. Princess Dellah is looking for an instructor to teach the soldiers Galactic Foreign Languages. The king plans to send more troops to Earth on assignment. They have to know how to properly assimilate with the Humans to avoid detection. I couldn't think of anyone better than Etienne."

Amos ducked his head to hide his tears. "Your generosity is too much."

General Iham looked at Gallium. "Your father has always been too modest!" Turning to Amos, he said, "I don't want to hear it! Go and tell your wife the good news. Princess Dellah's personal assistant will escort you to your new living quarters."

He turned to Gallium again. "Well, young MaleForm, I guess we'll be seeing a lot of each other. King Carlomon and Princess Dellah believe in keeping families together."

Gallium shook his outstretched hand. "Thank you for referring my ParentForms to the king. This will make my mother very happy."

The general's grip was firm. "It makes me happy too. This is a good move for Coldarius. With the upcoming merger, we have to keep our guard up."

Amos eyed him suspiciously. "What do you mean? Do you think King Dubian will go back on his word?"

General Iham's lips thinned. "No, it's not that. Everyone knows he's obsessed with marrying Princess Dellah. He'll do anything to make her happy. But I don't trust the little cretin."

He met Amos's eyes. "I barely heard him speak two words when King Anemi was alive. Now he barks orders as if he's been doing it all his life. The Platirian kings have always been evil. He puts on a good show in front of her, but I don't think he'll be any different. I'm thankful we have strong leadership. Unlike the Amorous royal family, they care about us. It sounds terrible, but as long as Princess Dellah is heading up the merger, I don't think we'll have anything to worry about."

"That's good to hear!" said Amos. "I trust her to do what's best for Coldarius."

"So do I," said General Iham. "Now, if you'll excuse me, I need to pick up some Springhalt for Lady Alarah. She's expecting again!"

Amos grabbed his hand, shaking furiously. "That's wonderful news! I'm so happy for you. I know how long you've tried to have another InfantForm."

"Congratulations," said Gallium.

Although he was happy for the general, he didn't care much for his wife. Her personality vastly differed from her husband's. While he was warm and friendly, she was arrogant and dismissive.

She thought her husband's position gave her the right to look down her nose at others. Gallium wondered how she'd feel after hearing his family had joined the king's personal circle.

"What will she have?" asked Amos.

General Iham's smile was wider than a WarCraft. "We're having a son."

Amos looked as if he wanted to say more, but thought better of it. General Iham was kind, intelligent, and blinded by love for his wife. Cognizant that they weren't a good match, he hoped she'd learn to reciprocate his affection.

Although Amos wondered when his friend would come to his senses, he respected him too much to in their marriage. Every Being had their own cross to bear—willingly or not.

Gallium rounded a curve and made the rest of the journey to the palace alone. Amos had hurried off to share news of their good fortune with Etienne. They'd only need their personal items—all furnishings would be provided in their new cottage.

Princess Dellah sent traveling staff to pack up their belongings to ease the hassle of the move. He thought her heart was just as beautiful as her face. He breathed in the fresh, crisp air. It was wonderful to be alive on Coldarius!

They had plenty to eat and no one lacked anything. Not only did the MaleForms and WomenForms love and respect each other, their royal family tolerated none of the misogyny and discrimination Platirius thrived on. He hoped things would never change.

Princess Dellah saw him as he rounded a curve. "Gallium!" she said, running toward him. "You've made it! I sent General Iham to tell your father the good news."

He returned her smile. "Yes, we met him in the middle of the square. I can't thank you enough for everything you've done for my family."

She winked at him. "Well, I'm afraid I have another surprise. When I move to Platirius, I'd like you to come with me. I'm appointing you as my chief royal gardener! What do you say?"

His mouth dropped. He assumed he'd stay on Coldarius and take orders from a distance. Now she wanted him to live on Platirius with her.

He bowed to her. "Saying I'm excited would be an understatement. Thank you, Princess Dellah. It's truly an honor."

She smiled up at him. "Platirius is attractive, but it lacks the natural beauty we have. I want to change that. In fact, now that King Anemi and Prince Dimaro are gone, I intend to bring proper order to many things on that planet."

He noted her determined look. He suspected she meant she'd put an end to how Platirian MaleForms treated the WomenForms. Since she was a staunch supporter of their rights, he was confident she'd turn things around. After all, she had King Dubian wrapped around her little finger. Gallium was very proud they were under her leadership.

"Take your things up to your cottage. I'll show you where I want you to begin after luncheon. Here's a list of flowers I'd like you to plant after you go to the dining chamber. I think they'd make the east wing look much better."

He took the list and read it. "I can get started right now."

She raised one petite finger in the air. "Only after you eat. I know you. Once you get started, you won't eat until you're finished. I promised Etienne I'd make sure you eat properly, and you will. That's an order."

They smiled at each other. "I'd be a fool to ignore that. Alright, I'll get the seeds after luncheon."

Just looking at her made him woozy.

She winked at him. "Good. I'll see you in a while."

He bowed while silently appreciating her curves as she walked away. He scanned the list again and was pleased to see she'd selected some of the most beautiful hybrid flowers he'd created. It would be fun to use his imagination to restructure the palace grounds.

He wondered if he'd see the lovely WomanForm who helped in her mother's flower shop. He looked forward to seeing her again. But for now, he had to put away his gear and get familiar with his new home.

It took a few hours to put away all his belongings. He smiled with satisfaction at the grand living and bed chambers with a connected bath chamber. A bonus gaming room, complete with the latest technology and gadgets, heightened his excitement.

A plush gaming chair sat in front of a large console. He wasn't surprised the cottage lacked a private dining chamber. All the royal servants ate together in the palace's expansive dining chamber. That was fine with him.

Although the king had a smaller private dining chamber, he and Princess Dellah preferred to eat with their subjects. They were loved for the humility and respect they showed everyone. Gallium placed a hand on his rumbling stomach. The royal dining staff were the best cooks on the planet. He was looking forward to seeing what was on the menu.

On his way to the dining chamber, he glanced at the beautifully decorated flower shop on the corner. Pausing to admire Amos's workmanship, he thought of the lovely sales clerk again. He'd find out if she was working, but at the moment, he was hungry.

Expecting an influx of new staff moving into the compound, the dining staff had outdone themselves. There were long trays of mashed potatoes with pools of butter swimming on top. Beings waited in line for juicy steaks—cooked to order.

He saw meatloaf, roast chicken, and stewed chicken swimming in gravy, cabbage with sausages and onions, roasted sweet corn that had been cut off the cob and simmered in butter, spices, and sugar, and scalloped potatoes simmering in a thick, creamy cheese sauce.

Platters of pork, lamb, and duck accompanied colorful vegetable and fruit salads. Dessert consisted of decadent chocolate, lemon, and coconut cakes. Pie lovers were pleased to find apple, peach, and cherry pies with an assortment of velvety ice cream.

Massive bowls of whipping cream and chocolate sauce waited at the end of the counter. The dining staff greeted him with a smile and heaped huge portions on his plate.

He politely thanked them for suggesting which desserts to try first. Opting to take a seat away from the energetic chatter buzzing about, he recited a short prayer before inhaling the wonderful aromas rising from his plate.

His first bite was sheer ecstasy. He thanked The One for caring enough about him to provide such an amazing blessing.

With a full belly and a grateful spirit, the flower shop was next on his list. To his delight, she stood at the counter ringing up an order. His breath caught when she looked up at him.

Her caramel-colored hair complemented eyes that reminded him of bars of gold. Her honey-brown skin looked soft enough to fall asleep on.

He took in her long eyelashes and full lips, captivated by the rounded, exquisite curves of her hips and thighs. She wasn't skinny, and that's precisely how he liked his WomenForms. She was a breathtaking sight.

He cleared his throat and nodded at her. "Hello, I'm Gallium."

Returning his nod, she said, "I know who you are. You're the new chief royal gardener."

He hoped his smile was charming enough to impress her. "Wow, word gets around fast. I just started today and you already know who I am? I'm impressed."

Her voice was low and soothing. "Everyone's been talking about the new MaleForm with the pretty green eyes. Coldarius is small, so everyone hears everything."

His gaze caressed her face. "I hope you've only heard good things then?"

She leaned against the counter on her elbow. "For now. But who you really are remains to be seen. What can I do for you?"

He cleared his throat again. He was glad she wasn't falling all over him. He appreciated a good chase. "I'll need some Aricoberry, Sholtzphatz, Manurim, Callebrame, and Dutzchopat."

She listened to him rattle off the list of seeds before retrieving them. Setting them on the counter, she said, "These are some of our best flowers. If Princess Dellah hired you, it means you know your way around plants."

Lifting a manicured nail in the air, she said, "But I'll warn you, mixing Callebrame and Dutzhopat is dangerous. They're not harmful on their own, but when they're mixed, Beings have been known to hallucinate and act out violently."

He fingered the tiny packages of seeds. "Yes, I know. I've been experimenting with plants for quite a while now."

She placed the bundles into a large sack before raising her palm in front of his outstretched hand. Once the funds were electronically transferred to her, she pushed the bag across the counter to him.

"Then you also know to protect yourself while working with them? Some of the oils may produce terrible reactions on your skin."

He flashed another dazzling smile at her. "Oh, yes. I'm aware. Are you a medical student? You seem to know a lot about hazardous side effects."

She shook her head. "No. Blame it on years of experience."

Feeling the heat of his penetrating gaze, she looked away. The WomenForms were correct for once—this one was exceptionally tall, handsome, and well-built. He wore his thick black hair long and pulled away from his blemish-free face.

She struggled to keep her knees from buckling when his sea-green eyes looked into hers. Now wasn't the time to act like a silly colt in front of him.

She prided herself on building a reputation for having intellect and physical strength. She had no intentions of putting her dreams of joining King Carlomon's army on hold for marriage. Most MaleForms moved on once they realized she wasn't interested in entertaining them.

She gave them no more thought than a bird landing on a branch—but he was different. She'd noticed him just as much as he'd noticed her, and found she wasn't able to brush off thoughts of him so easily. She'd awakened with remnants of fiery dreams licking at her psyche on more than a few nights.

"I've seen you around, but I've never had the chance to ask your name."

She stared at him pensively for a long time. "My name is Legend."

Chapter 2

O nce word got out about the new chief royal gardener's talent, Coldarians and even Platirians came to see his work. At first, the senior gardening staff were reluctant to take orders from a MaleForm so young. However, they were eager to follow his lead once they witnessed firsthand how plants flourished under his tutelage.

Soon, Coldarius's landscaping was the envy of every kingdom in the galaxy. King Carlomon received bids to allow Gallium to travel to other realms to help revitalize their lands.

Princess Dellah turned down every request. She had commissioned him to beautify the grounds of Coldarius and her soon-to-be new home, Platirius. She intended for her wedding to be the talk of the galaxy for years to come.

He'd promised that the gardens she'd take her nuptials in would be the most exquisite anyone had ever seen. She had no time to lend him to other nations. At least not for a while.

In the future, she planned to use his skills as a bargaining chip to secure resources from other planets that Coldarius and Platirius lacked. Expanding two empires simultaneously wasn't easy, but she was more than ready for the task.

She grew nervous as her wedding day approached. Platirius was very different from Coldarius. While the Beings she'd known all her life were warm and friendly, the Platirians were wary and distrustful.

Malicious gossip permeated through the various chambers. She suspected King Dubian wasn't well liked and, by association, neither was she. Changing the disastrous reputation set by King Anemi and his predecessors was crucial to making the Platirians feel as loved and respected as her subjects.

She was glad his reign had finally ended. Although she was displeased to hear rumors it was by her fiancé's hand, it was a relief not to be forced to deal with him—or Prince Dimaro. Had he lived, their marriage would've been disastrous.

After King Anemi discovered she'd been seeing Dubian, he quickly sabotaged their impending engagement and convinced her father that his eldest son would be a better match.

During their first meeting, she'd found him to be arrogant and disrespectful. She politely deflated his enormous ego and left him and his father standing with their mouths hanging open.

Neither were used to headstrong WomenForms. Still, King Anemi was determined to push through with the merger. He informed her his second son would marry her over his dead body. Ironically, that's precisely what happened.

In her eyes, her intended was kind and charming. But the rumors had spun out of control. Some were convinced he was just as ignoble as his father. At times, she wondered if he was trying to deceive her. She supposed time would tell.

General Sodom had been King Anemi's right hand. Her first order of business was to have him replaced by General Iham. If she expected to turn things around, she'd need her most trusted supporters at her side. Overall, the benefits stemming from the marriage outweighed the losses.

The merger would be lucrative for everyone. Most importantly, she'd marry out of love, not duty. As time passed, she hoped everyone would see him as she did. Shaking off the fear that crept upon her, she looked forward to her upcoming nuptials.

G allium was also looking forward to the wedding—he wanted it to be over. He'd been working in the royal gardening chamber since dawn. It was well after supper time before he stood and rolled his aching neck. Princess Dellah wanted two thousand roses at her wedding—half blue and half platinum.

They were to cover the grounds of the new wedding chamber his father had finished building the previous month. It rivaled the chamber that had stood since Platirius's early days.

Rows of silver pews stood behind a lavish stage complete with a podium and the most advanced technical gadgets. Immediately after King Anemi's death, King Dubian ordered the old one to be demolished. He hadn't wanted to marry in the same place as his father and grandfather.

It was no coincidence very little of the structures commissioned by King Anemi remained. After assuming the throne, he sought to erase his father's legacy. He was adamant that every chamber be demolished or restructured. Gone were the melancholy gray walls and highly polished onyx floors.

Since the princess's favorite color was blue, he ordered the decorators and builders to design every chamber according to her specifications. No stone was left untouched. Everyone was put on notice—a new reign had come to Platirius. Nothing would be as it was.

Gallium rubbed his sore neck. He'd spent hours getting items ready to be transported to Platirius. It was his responsibility to plan every detail of the massive wedding garden. The task was more challenging than anything he'd ever faced, but he was determined not to disappoint Princess Dellah.

Etienne stepped inside and looked around. "Wow... I've never seen so many gorgeous plants in my lifespan!" Assessing him with a critical gaze, she said, "It looks as if you could use a break, young MaleForm. I had second-guessed coming to see you, but I think my timing is perfect." Smiling, she held up a basket. "I packed all your favorites. Let's go outside and eat, hm?"

He stretched his arms. His broad shoulders were screaming for relief. "I'll gladly take you up on that."

After they washed their hands, she spread a white blanket on the soft blue grass and gestured for him to sit. Together, they removed the contents from the basket. There was a small selection of smooth, delectable cheeses, clusters of crisp, juicy grapes, ripe strawberries, a loaf of soft bread, and thinly sliced roast beef and turkey.

He was surprised when she uncovered a freshly baked chicken pie filled with plump pieces of chicken, carrots, peas, and pearl onions swimming in cream sauce and thick slices of chocolate cake. A thermos of wine would wash down the bounty.

He marveled at the amount of food. "Mother, did you think you were feeding me and all the staff assigned under me?"

She took a bite of bread and cheese. "I didn't know who would be here with you, and I didn't want anyone to feel left out. No worries. I'll pack up what we don't finish and place it in your new ice box. I hurried to buy one when Amos told me you didn't have a private dining chamber. It keeps me from worrying about you skipping meals."

She observed the starter plants he'd begun working on. "The blue roses are so pretty! And you planted rainbow ones too!"

"Yes, Princess Dellah wants blue ones at her wedding. I'm almost finished packing up the seeds. They don't take long to grow to full maturity—one to three days at the most." He spread cheese on a slice of bread. "These won't be ordinary roses. They'll be bigger than a Coldarian's head. If I do everything right, I'll make a name for myself. I'm happy the princess allowed me to be a part of it."

She nibbled on a strawberry. "You'll be successful—you're too talented not to be. If they're the size of your father's head, they'll be large enough to sit on." That made him laugh, but her tone turned serious. "She selected the very best—you. Never doubt yourself or your talent. This wedding will certainly be a long feather in your cap."

She cupped his cheek. "Your father and I are so proud The One has blessed you with a unique gift."

She cut a large piece of the pie and served it to him. "It's only right for you to show everyone how talented you are. I hear King Hitam wants to hire you to design gold roses to celebrate his daughter's birth. He told King Carlomon he's willing to pay handsomely for them."

He took a bite of pie and nodded. "I'd like to, but it'll have to wait until after the wedding. That's my first priority."

She frowned. "King Dubian is certainly sparing no expense. He gave Amos a list of demands for how he wanted each chamber to look. There are over two hundred chambers on Platirius. I can't believe he wanted all of them changed or rebuilt." She shook her head. "He must've really hated his father."

He tossed one of the grapes into his mouth. "I work for Princess Dellah, not him. After they marry, I doubt he'll order me around."

She passed him a glass of wine. "Wait for it. He orders everyone around. He's nothing like King Carlomon. He has no respect for anyone except Princess Dellah. He's careful to keep the mask on when she's around, but when she's not, he's just as mean-spirited and spiteful as the rest of his family. His subjects loathe the ground he walks on. I just hope it doesn't carry over to her. She doesn't deserve backlash because of his disgusting ways."

He swirled the wine in the glass. "No, she doesn't. She has a golden heart and a kind nature. The Platirians are in for a swift reckoning if they think they'll run over her. She stood in as our general before General Iham was appointed. I've never seen a WomanForm fight like that."

She laughed and clapped her hands. "Oh yes, they'll soon find out our princess has a spine of steel. Who would be better than she to straighten out those nasty Platirians? Especially the MaleForms. They have no respect for WomenForms, but I think that'll change once she becomes the new queen."

He drained the goblet and held it out for more wine. "What happened to King Anemi's wife?"

"She married a younger MaleForm on another planet. She didn't have the decency to wait until his body was cold. That entire family is disgraceful."

They finished their supper and tidied up the mess. As promised, she collected the leftovers and placed them in the icebox.

He signed with contentment. "Thanks for the food, Mother. I really needed a break."

She kissed his cheek. "The sooner you finish your project, the better you'll feel. I won't be back for a while. Teaching the soldiers is more labor intensive than teaching small ChildForms. I was surprised by how many signed up for my course. I had to open more slots, but I'm not complaining. The pay is excellent and I make my own schedule. Be sure to take breaks when you can. You're no use to the princess if you wear yourself out."

"Yes, Mother. I will. Tell Father I'll visit when I have time."

She nodded. "In a while," she said.

Coldarians never said goodbye. It was considered poor etiquette to suggest you'd never see a Being again.

Engrossed in his work, Gallium didn't realize he had another visitor. He looked up and stared into the dark eyes of King Dubian. Quickly, he rose and bowed before him.

"Good evening, Your Highness. This is very unexpected. Are you looking for Princess Dellah?"

It was difficult to read his blank expression. His eyes slowly traveled from Gallium's feet to the top of his head. "Why would I expect to find my fiancée here?"

He hadn't missed the thinly veiled venom in the king's tone. It became clear why he was hated—he was rude and discourteous.

"She expressed how she wanted the gardens to look for the wedding. We've been working closely together to make sure everything meets her expectations."

King Dubian picked up a black rose, sniffing deeply. "How closely? Is she here after sunset?"

What is he going on about? thought Gallium. "The Princess is never anywhere except the palace after dark. We have strict security measures here."

"I hear you're an expert in turning plants into substances. What exactly do you do for King Carlomon?"

"That information is classified. I'm unable to inform you of any assignments I complete for him."

He raised an eyebrow. "After you transition to Platirius, you'll be under my command. I expect my questions to be answered immediately."

If he could've gotten away with it, Gallium would've tossed him out of his home like a sack of wheat. He was disrespectful, dismissive, and extremely arrogant.

He resented how the king spoke to him—as if he were an ant who needed his permission to crawl across the floor. Getting a grip on his temper, he chose his words carefully. It wouldn't do to show insolence to a royal—especially Princess Dellah's groom.

Was it jealousy that caused King Dubian to seek him out and size him up? If so, that was ridiculous. Although he couldn't understand why she'd chosen to marry him, Gallium didn't question her loyalty. There was no need to suspect her of cheating. His mother had been right—he didn't deserve her.

He rubbed a hand over his beard. "Yes, Your Highness. *After* I move to Platirius, I'll happily answer your questions."

The king's empty orbits looked through him. "But you're failing to answer them now."

Gallium shook his head. "I haven't failed at anything. This is Coldarius. I'm under King Carlomon's command."

Noting the ice in his tone, King Dubian took a step toward him. If he meant for his cold smile to be intimidating, it wasn't. "You Coldarians really have veins of steel, don't you? Could it be the cold weather you deal with all year round?"

What a creepy creature, thought Gallium. "I think it has more to do with having a princess who teaches us how to *deal* with things. Our weather is the least of our concerns. It's a part of us. Cold, brilliant, and resilient. It is who we are and who we'll always be."

His smile was frozen in place. He wasn't pleased he'd lost the upper hand with Gallium. He was used to Beings cowering before him. But his bold stare and flippant tongue proved his status hadn't impressed him.

He despised the handsome Coldarian. He was much too good-looking, brave, and strong—everything he wasn't.

King Dubian was ugly and he knew it. His oddly shaped, squarish body had averted more than a few of the WomenForm's eyes. His skin would never be as clear and his eyes were too wide.

He hated to admit Princess Dellah looked better on Gallium's arm than his. He didn't want him coming to Platirius. Just the thought of his beloved smiling at him churned his stomach.

What he lacked in physical beauty, he made up with subterfuge. Trying to convince her to leave him behind would raise too many red flags.

For now, he had to treat the Coldarians—especially Gallium—respectfully. Otherwise, his plans would blow up in his face. He couldn't afford to take the chance that she'd call off the engagement.

"Your loyalty to Princess Dellah and her father is something to be admired—er—what did you say your name was?"

He hid his distaste at his attempt to minimize the significance of his existence. The king knew exactly who he was and they both knew it.

He sat down and picked up a pair of pruning shears. "It's Gallium. It's easy to remember. I'm the only one on your planet and mine who grows plants impressive enough to please your fiancée."

King Dubian took a step backward. "Yes...well...I don't think I'll ever forget you, Gallium."

Gallium's beautiful smile held a hint of frost. "No, I don't think you will. I wish you a grand night...Your Highness."

Infuriated by the gardener's dismissive tone, he pictured him raw and bleeding, carelessly stuffed inside a death craft. "And you as well, Gallium. We'll meet again soon."

A few seconds of silence passed between the MaleForms. "I look forward to it."

Scowling, King Dubian left him, his eyes as black as the night.

"A rainbow rose!" said Legend. She took it from Gallium's extended hand. "You really are a master of making gorgeous things, aren't you?"

She smelled its sweet fragrance and sighed. "It's so pretty!" She found a crystal container to fill with water and placed a small patch of plant food inside. Then carefully settled the rose into the water before stepping back to admire it.

"Hmm. It looks lonely," he said. "Here's some friends to keep it company."

He pulled eleven rainbow roses from behind his back and presented them to her.

She looked up at him in wonder. "It's too much!" she cried. "They're too beautiful!"

"Not as beautiful as you. When I saw how great they turned out, I had to run over and give them to you."

She looked longingly at the beautiful bouquet. "I thought Princess Dellah had you growing acres of flowers for her wedding."

He shrugged. "That's true, but I'm good at juggling multiple tasks."

She added the additional roses to the vase and smiled. "Well, I'll take these as my going away gift."

His heart plummeted. "Going away? To where?"

Her golden eyes sparkled with mischief. "I've applied to join Platirius's army."

His grip tightened on the counter. "You've already signed up to be a soldier for Coldarius. Why would you want to go to Platirius when they treat WomenForms so badly?"

She shrugged. "It would be a pay increase. I could send enough money home so my MotherForm wouldn't have to work so hard in her flower shop. She could close it down or sell it—whatever she chose. King Carlomon pays well, but Platirius is richer than Coldarius. That's why we're merging with them."

While he understood her motive, he didn't think it was worth being mistreated by the Platirians.

"Then wait for the merger. Once that happens, Coldarius's economy will expand and we'll be on the same level as Platirius. You could stay here and be treated with respect."

She pouted. "You're going to Platirius. What makes it okay for you?"

"I don't have to worry about some crazy MaleForm forcing himself on me."

Immediately, her hand went to her hip. "I'm a good soldier who can hold my own. I'm not some weakling who needs protection."

He held up a hand in surrender. "I know that. I didn't mean to imply you can't handle yourself. It's just..." He sighed in frustration.

She cocked her head. "It's just what?"

"I care about you. I'd lose my head if some MaleForm placed his filthy hands on you. Platirians have been crazy all their lifespans. I don't want to see you get hurt."

She fingered one of the delicate petals of the roses. "Your concern is appreciated. But if I'm selected to go to Platirius, I'm going. I'll work hard to rise in the ranks. I'm going to be Platirius's first WomanForm general."

His brows shot up. "A WomanForm general? On Platirius? That's never happened."

The playful sassiness in her gaze made him regret what he was about to say, but it needed to be said. Platirius was the last place she should be.

"With General Sodom running things over there, it never will."

She was undeterred. "Princess Dellah is taking General Iham with her."

"Yes, but he still has to co-command the armies with General Sodom. King Dubian won't allow his general to be replaced. He's won too many battles for him. Like it or not, there's a reason Platirius has one of the best militaries around."

She crossed her arms over her chest. "So does Coldarius. It doesn't matter what you say. I'm not changing my mind."

He sighed. "Okay, fine. Let's not talk about it anymore. I have to get back anyway."

She nodded. "I know how busy you are these days."

He plucked a few of the petals and placed them in her hair. "Yeah, but I wanted to take some time and see you. You're important to me."

A smile peaked out. "Hey, don't mess up my new friends or my hair. It took me a long time to get it to look this good."

His eyes glowed with satisfaction. "You always look great."

She playfully saluted him. "Thank you for the beautiful roses. In a while."

He bowed to her. "In a while, Legend."

"Hey, I'm not royalty!"

He opened the door and turned back to her. "You are to me."

She couldn't bring herself to speak. She watched until he rounded the curve leading away from the shop. Guiding her finger across the roses again, she thought of a new future involving a life on Platirius. And...a life with Gallium.

King Carlomon sat in his impressive meeting chamber with King Dubian, finalizing the plans to consolidate their resources. The young king's energy gave him hope that his decision to join forces was solid. On many occasions, he'd proven he was committed to marrying his daughter.

He rapidly held up his palm as King Dubian drafted his signature on the documents.

"You're not reading the fine print. I think it's imperative that you're fully aware of what we're signing today."

He smiled at the older king. "There's no need. Whatever Princess Dellah wants, she'll have. Our wedding is in a couple days, and I'm eager to finish our business so I can focus on that. Nothing is more important than making my future bride happy."

King Carlomon raised his palm for the final time, returning his smile. "I'm happy she's found such a strong MaleForm like you to take care of her."

King Dubian laughed. "Don't let her hear you say that. She was born to take heads. I don't think she'd be happy to hear she needs to be taken care of."

Taking a sip of wine, King Carlomon said, "That much is true, but even the strongest Beings need help sometimes—even my daughter. I have no doubt she will help lead Platirius to an even greater empire than it is now. I've always found two is better than one."

"That's sound wisdom. I'm honored she accepted my proposal. She'll be a much better queen than Queen Zherta."

He noted the hint of bitterness that had crept into King Dubian's tone. "I thought things were amicable between you and your MotherForm. Have you been in contact with her? Will she attend the wedding?"

"No," he said quietly. "I've already informed Princess Dellah I don't want her there. She understands and respects my wishes."

King Carlomon traced the code for *send* on his palm. All the documents they'd signed were now encrypted safely into King Dubian's personal electronic system. "Well, so do I. I'm sure it hasn't been easy being King Anemi's son, but you've turned out to be a better MaleForm than him."

Surprised, he looked up at him. "Thank you. That's very generous of you."

"I mean it. I wouldn't say I liked the way your father treated her or any of the WomenForms under his care. However, you cherish my daughter in the way I've always hoped she would be—with tenderness and love. I couldn't ask for a better son-in-law."

King Dubian smiled wryly. "It's too bad I don't have the looks of that new gardener. The One was in a generous mood when He created him, don't you think?"

Surprised, King Carlomon cocked his head. "Who? Gallium? Ah, yes...he's a strapping brute. We've had to put extra security in place to keep the young WomenForms away from the gardening chamber so he could work in peace. But looks aren't everything, and my daughter has never been so shallow to be blinded by what's on the surface."

"I'm grateful to her. And to you and Queen Elia for rearing her to be such a fine WomanForm."

"I look forward to spoiling the grand ChildForms you and my daughter will give me."

A dark, fleeting look passed in his eyes. It was so quick, King Carlomon convinced himself he'd imagined it. An uncomfortable silence passed between them.

"I think...we'll only need a Firstborn. I see no reason to have more than that. Second ChildForms can sometimes be unwanted burdens."

"What do you mean?"

He pasted a bright, false smile on his face. "I want my future wife to have all the freedom she needs to make her dreams come true. I don't intend to stand in the way of her plans. That's all I meant."

He rubbed his hands together in anticipation. "Now, you promised to give me a tour of your kingdom. I've been looking forward to it all day. I'm very interested in eating in your new dining chamber. Once I see it, I may have some ideas for ours. I purposely left the redecorating on the back burner."

"Of course. I don't know about you, but I'm hungrier than a bear. Come, let me show you our home."

But as he led him out of the meeting chamber, a tiny wave of dread crept over him. King Dubian's mood had drastically changed when he mentioned Queen Zherta and having multiple ChildForms.

Although his support of Princess Dellah's ambitions was admirable, King Carlomon couldn't help wondering if there was something more to it.

He shook his head.

You're being silly.

All too soon, he would be family. If King Dubian wanted to lighten the load for his daughter, who was he to interfere? He quickly set his fears aside and stepped into the cold, biting air. By the time they reached the center of town, he'd forgotten his strange demeanor.

"And here's one of the places our gardening chamber provides the plants to sell to the community. I know I'm bragging when I say Zita's Blossoms has the best flowers around, but it's true. I have fresh bouquets delivered every morning."

King Dubian stepped inside and looked around. The small store had an impressive display of flowers and plants. Many of the jardinières were the most elegant he'd ever seen. He coveted some of them for the grand halls of his palace. He spotted a WomanForm standing at the counter and stopped. She looked vaguely familiar.

"Hello, I'm King Dubian. I'm Princess Dellah's groom."

Legend bowed to King Carlomon before turning to bow to him. "Good afternoon, King Carlomon. Yes, everyone knows who you are, King Dubian. We're all excited for the wedding."

His contemptuous onyx gaze sent a chill down her spine. "I'm amazed to see a Platirian working on Coldarius. Did you apply for a work pass?"

Legend and King Carlomon frowned. "I'm not a Platirian. I'm a Coldarian," she said.

He stopped short. "Oh? Please accept my apologies. I could've sworn you were a Platirian. Your look is very exotic for a Coldarian."

She raised an eyebrow but didn't question him. It was forbidden for a commoner to question a royal.

King Dubian met King Carlomon's confused gaze. "You see, most Coldarian WomenForms have eyes the color of the seas or silver like Princess Dellah's. But her eyes are gold. On Platirius, our WomenForms' eyes are either gold or multi-colored. And in rare cases, they're black like mine."

"Ah, I see," said King Carlomon, although he didn't see how he'd drawn the conclusion on such a finite issue. "Actually, I've never thought of it. But I assure you, Legend is one of us. I remember the day she was born. I appreciate your apology. It's very kind of you."

It was extremely rare for a Platirian royal to apologize to a commoner, but he'd craftily copied the mannerisms of the princess. On Platirius, he apologized to no one.

Growing up shunned and alone, he'd learned to play roles that differed from his true nature. He thought it would put him in a good light to appear more humble than he was. Legend was shocked she could read his thoughts.

"It's my pleasure to apologize to such a lovely WomanForm," he said, smiling at her.

No, it isn't, she thought.

Had King Carlomon not been standing at his side, she was certain she wouldn't have received an apology.

But how did I know what he was thinking?

Smiling proudly at her, King Carlomon said, "Legend has applied to join Platirius's army. I would hate to lose her, but knowing she'd be on Platirius to guard my daughter would help me sleep much better."

His chilling leer swept over her again. "We've never had WomenForms in our army," he said quietly. "I'll need to speak with General Sodom about it."

His tone told her she wouldn't be joining his army—not now or ever.

Feeling the slight chill in the room, King Carlomon looked from him to her. "Were you aware my daughter was once the General of Coldarius?"

She smiled inwardly. She was proud that her king believed in equality for WomenForms.

King Dubian's calm facade finally cracked. He turned and stared at King Carlomon. "My Dellah fought MaleForms?"

King Carlomon nodded smugly. "Not only did she fight, she's killed a great number of them. She trained Legend and some of the other WomenForms here. General Sodom has an impeccable record, but Princess Dellah is interested in getting better acquainted with Platirius's military."

King Dubian blinked. Trying to picture his fiancée in armor was difficult. "Well...I'll discuss it with her after the wedding." He turned to her, who didn't miss the note of disdain shimmering in his eyes. "It was nice meeting you, Legend."

She nodded. "And you as well, Your Highness."

She stifled a sigh of relief when King Carlomon excused them and headed for the dining chamber. To her, King Dubian was as creepy as they came. And repulsive. She mouthed a silent prayer for Princess Dellah. She'd certainly need all the grace of The One to deal with someone like him.

Mrs. Guilde appeared quietly from the back of the store. "Are they gone?"

Legend noted the trembling in her voice. "Mother? What's wrong? Yes, they just left, and I thank The One if I never have to see him again. He makes me nauseous." Her eyes brightened. "Mother! I can read his thoughts! How is that possible?"

Mrs. Guilde gazed at her sadly. "There's a reason for that. Come and sit down, Legend. There's something I have to tell you. I hoped I never would, but now...I can't avoid it any longer." She nodded at the door. "Turn the *Closed* sign over."

Legend did as she was told and sat down with her. Quietly, Mrs. Guilde began pulling back the ribbons on a past she'd tried desperately to forget.

King Dubian was envious of the dining chamber. In comparison, the one inside his palace was antiquated. When he returned to Platirius, he'd order the gardener's father to build the most extravagant one anyone had ever seen. Deeply rooted insecurities wouldn't allow him to be outshone by the Coldarians.

He wanted Platirius to be the number one show of power and wealth. He stared grudgingly at the menu. The dining staff was well prepared for his arrival. They'd worked hard to provide the very best dishes. And it delighted them to show the Platirians they had steep competition.

The kings were served pan-seared scallops in truffle oil, jumbo prawns, and a savory rice dish with creamy herbed butter. Medium-rare steaks sat aside twice-baked potatoes, crisp asparagus with parmesan and bacon, and the largest, pillowy-soft rolls King Dubian had ever bit into.

He'd never heard of some of the dressings for the vegetable salad, but the samples he drizzled over the tender leaves were extraordinary. He groaned in delight when the honey butter he slathered on the rolls melted in his mouth. Boards of highly polished wood held elaborate displays of thinly sliced meats, cheeses, and fresh fruit.

He made a mental note to fire any of Platirius's dining staff who couldn't exceed the culinary skills of King Carlomon's staff.

On Platirius, Princess Dellah was having a luncheon of a different kind—with the heads of Platirius's chambers. Wanting to ensure she got off on the right foot with the Platirians, she'd summoned them together for an important meeting. As their future queen, it was imperative for everyone to be clear on her expectations.

She sat in King Dubian's high chair, allowing her feet to dangle underneath the enormous desk. "Thank you all for coming today. I know how busy you are, so I'll get right to the point. There is far too much in-fighting and gossiping going on. Not only within the work chambers, but inside the palace as well. I've heard that not only did King Anemi and Queen Zherta make no effort to stop it, they encouraged it. That will no longer be the case."

She looked around at the crowd to make sure she had their attention. "On Coldarius, we live and work as one unit. As a team. We do not have time, nor have my father and I ever made time, for pettiness. We all know I wasn't born on Platirius. However, I will become a Platirian very soon."

Holding their stares with ease, she said, "Let me assure you, I intend for the peaceful harmony Coldarians enjoy to be extended to Platirius as well. For the first time in history, I will select a group of my trusted staff to accompany me to live here. I expect nothing less than harmonious relationships fostered between Coldarians and Platirians."

Some of the Platirians began whispering among themselves. They'd expected her to be a meek, self-depreciating WomanForm who would do King Dubian's bidding without question. They had just discovered they were wrong.

She waited for the whispering and shifting around to stop. "As of today, I'm issuing a no gossiping decree. No longer will Beings be forced to suffer under malicious gossip and shattered reputations. If one has grounds for slander, the tormentor will be called to stand in before the justice council. If one is found guilty of slander, the victim will be awarded everything you own. And I mean everything."

Shocked, angry glares darted at her as furious whispers spread among the spectators. She ignored them. "If you cannot prove what you say or have nothing nice to say about your neighbors, then it's best to say nothing at all."

Ana Weiss chuckled maliciously. "I have nothing nice to say about any of you," she whispered. A few evil chuckles rang out among her small group of supporters.

"What's that you said, Ana Weiss?" asked Princess Dellah. "If you have something relevant to add, then please stand and say it to my face."

Ana gasped. She didn't think the princess had heard her. Haughtily, she stood. "I meant no disrespect, Princess Dellah."

Princess Dellah's silver eyes resembled chips of ice. "Then what did you mean, Ana? Obviously, it was important enough to rudely interrupt my meeting. I'd like to hear you make your statement out loud."

Ana bristled, clearly offended by the princess's imperious tone. "It's not that serious, Your Highness," she said frostily.

The spectators looked from Ana to Princess Dellah. Ana was related to General Sodom. That made Beings fear her. She knew it and willfully used it to her advantage. Everyone waited to see if her boldness would place the first crack in the princess's power. They didn't have to wait long.

"The only thing I see frivolous here is you," said Princess Dellah coldly.

A few gasps let out in the crowd.

"Silence," she hissed. "I don't want to hear another sound." Her eyes found Ana again. The fierceness in them made Ana unconsciously take a step back.

"Now, you may think your family's position gives you power, but let me assure you, I have no problem shipping you and your entire lot off Platirius. And if you don't think I'll do it, I invite you to test the limits of *my* power."

Ana's face clouded in fury. She pointed at her. "You're not the Queen of Platirius yet! You're a Coldarian. You have no business telling us what to do or when to do it! If you want to control something, stay in your place until you marry King Dubian. Until then, the little power you *think* you have only exists in your pretty little head."

Princess Dellah rose from the impressive desk. "Oh? You think so? Well, if that's what's going on in your confused, *decrepit* head, allow me to get you and everyone here straight. Right now. Guards."

Immediately, three Platirian soldiers appeared. "Yes, Princess Dellah? How may we be of service?"

She pointed to Ana. "Drag her out of this chamber and get her into a craft. Then, I want you to root out everyone related to her—and I do mean everyone—except General Sodom—and toss them into the craft with her."

Eyes blazing, she turned to Ana. "We're about to find out whether I *think* I have power or whether I *know* I do. I want everyone cleared out of here and standing at the center of the palace in five minutes." She scanned the crowd. "Don't make me come looking for you."

The crowd quickly cleared out of the meeting chamber, tripping over each other to get to the door. The soldiers grabbed Ana and forcibly ushered her and her family into a craft.

A few of the Coldarian soldiers who had accompanied the Princess stood by awaiting her orders. "Where shall we program the craft to go, Princess Dellah?" asked General Iham.

She held up a hand and turned to a visibly shaken General Sodom. "Do you have anything to say, General Sodom?"

He coughed and shook his head furiously. "No, Princess Dellah! Before King Dubian left for Coldarius, he said you're in charge of the military. I answer only to you!"

She nodded. "That's a good dog, Sodom."

She turned back to face Ana. Terrified, she stared out a window at her. Princess Dellah's deadly gaze never wavered from the older WomanForm. She said, "General Sodom, send that craft into the sun."

He saluted her. "Yes, Your Highness!"

Ana screamed when the craft powered up for launch. The startled Platirians watched in horror as it lifted into the air and flew rapidly toward the sun. The screams of terror subsided when it sank into the sun and burst into flames. She smiled and turned back to the crowd.

"My gossip decree will be enforced starting today. Anything said against a royal family member or any show of force against one shall be considered treason and will be met with immediate death. In either case, no trial will be heard before the justice council. You and your entire families will be tossed into the Flames of Justice or—" she looked at the sun again "—introduced to my new favorite way of taking out the trash—burned in the heart of the sun."

Waves of shock reverberated between the Platirians as they met her chilly gaze. "I have an abundance of respect for you Platirians. I want you to respect me too." Her brilliant platinum eyes sliced through the crowd. "But I wouldn't test the limits of my patience. The consequences...may prove to be fatal. Does anyone else have something to add?"

No one dared to breathe as she waited. She nodded. "Very well, you may return to your duties. I'm looking forward to a new Platirius—one that is prosperous and joyous for all of us. Those who do not understand my vision needn't worry about staying around to see it. Have I been heard?"

The Platirians didn't hesitate. "Yes, Princess Dellah!"

She flashed a dazzling smile at them. "Thank you for allowing me to join Platirius. I am looking forward to building a new reign with King Dubian."

Chapter 3

The wedding of King Dubian and Princess Dellah was the most spectacular event of the season. Their guests cheered as the newly crowned Queen of Platirius kissed her king under a bower of blue and platinum roses.

Only her extraordinarily lavish wedding gown overshadowed Gallium's arrangements of roses in colors and textures never seen before. The train was made of thousands of tiny diamonds and expanded across half the length of the palace's main entrance way.

To complement the queen's beauty, Gallium strategically placed roses made of pure diamonds along the edges of the aisle. As planned, they accented her gown as King Carlomon escorted her to the altar.

Although the borders had been opened for every Coldarian to attend, access to the wedding by other realms was by invitation only. The invitees watched in awe as the king whirled his new wife around the platinum floors of the wedding chamber.

The best wine and other spirits flowed freely as platters of shrimp, lobster, scallops, crab cakes, caviar, trout, and sea bass were devoured. One half of the dining chamber had rows of tables laden with samples of various hot and cold vegetable dishes, pasta, brisket, steak, and multiple chicken dishes.

The white wedding cake, frosted in platinum and edible sugar crystals replicating diamonds to match the bride's gown, was twelve layers high. She cheered as she and the groom cut into it, giving each other a hefty bite from their fingertips.

The platinum cutlery and sparkling dinnerware were the envy of every royal wife in attendance. They admired tablecloths made of the finest silk with embroidered diamonds around the base. But the most magnificent sight was the centerpieces.

Gallium had carefully arranged miniature blue roses around petite fountains made of hand-carved crystal angels. Sparkling-clear water mixed with diamonds flowed out of the angels' mouths. Everyone wondered how he was able to design such dazzling art.

Etienne joined him to watch the new royal couple whirling on the dance floor. She gave his arm a gentle squeeze. "Gallium, you have surpassed your own talent. This is the most breathtaking wedding I've ever seen."

He smiled. "Thank you, Mother. I put a lot of hard work into making sure Queen Dellah would be happy today."

"I know that, and everyone here knows it too. They haven't stopped talking about you growing roses out of diamonds! You'll be booked for the rest of your lifespan!"

He took it all in stride. "Only when and if she doesn't need me. I don't mind traveling to other realms. It'll give us lots of exposure."

Lady Alarah sauntered over to them. "I guess it's good Queen Dellah extended an open invite to all Coldarians," she said snootily. Looking into Etienne's eyes, she said, "Otherwise, some lowly souls couldn't have afforded to get in."

Etienne raised an eyebrow. "And who here is lowly, Lady Alarah? I don't see any Beings above anyone except for King Carlomon, Queen Dellah, and King Dubian."

Lady Alarah smiled craftily. "You've only been on King Carlomon's payroll for a short while. Your husband has worked with his hands all his life. Surely you don't think the king's money makes you smell any sweeter than a rose dipped in cow's excrement."

Gallium stiffened but Etienne discreetly touched his arm. "Well, if anyone knows how excrement smells, it would be you. Before you married General Iham, you fed the pigs your father had to raise after he gambled away the family fortune. It's too bad you snubbed King Carlomon before the throne passed to him. You could've had a royal wedding too."

She lifted her glass as if to throw its contents in her face, but Etienne said, "But The One knows best. He sent the perfect WomanForm to win his heart. Queen Elia was better than you at just about everything she did."

She looked over at Queen Dellah. "I doubt you would've given him a daughter as beautiful as that. Thank goodness Lyric looks exactly like General Iham. Otherwise, we might not have known who the father was."

Lady Alarah sputtered. "Why you!"

"Now let's be serious, *Lady* Alarah," said Etienne, slightly emphasizing *lady*. "You were a whore when we were growing up and you still are. I don't think you have room to talk about who smells sweet. Especially after my son told me you've been prescribed Sulphinite quite often."

Gallium cleared his throat and scanned the worship chamber for eavesdroppers. Sulphinite was used to treat sexually transmitted infections.

"And before you report him for slander, your personal physician told him. She hates you. I guess copulating with her husband wasn't the brightest idea, hm?"

Etienne took a sip of wine. "Gallium, this is the most refreshing wine I've ever tasted!" She lifted the glass to her nose. "And it smells so *sweet*!"

"You'll pay for this, Etienne Barrios," snarled Lady Alarah.

Etienne clucked her tongue, watching her storm off. "It's a shame such a beautiful wedding has such ugly hearts in attendance. Now, what were we talking about before we were so rudely interrupted? Oh yes. Your newfound fame. I'll need your autograph in advance, please?"

He shook his head and laughed. "Mother, you never cease to amaze me."

She batted her eyelashes. "What did I say?" She eyed Legend walking toward them in a beautiful gold ballgown. "I'm thinking maybe you'll get some new ideas for your own wedding."

He almost spilled his drink. Just in time, he set it down on a table and looked at her. "What in the galaxy are you talking about, Mother? I'm not getting married!"

"Oh? You think not?" She nodded toward Legend.

His eyes popped out of their sockets when he saw her. "Mother," he groaned.

She laughed and embraced the young WomanForm. "Hello, Legend! How are you?"

Legend returned her hug. "I'm on the moon looking at all the lovely flower arrangements your son made. And the fountains? By The One, I've never seen anything so beautiful!"

"Well, you're not too shabby yourself tonight," said Etienne.

"Oh, thank you, Mrs. Barrios. You look absolutely exquisite."

She gave Gallium a saucy wink. "We Coldarians clean up well, don't we?"

He ignored his mother's knowing glance. "Definitely."

"Ah, I think I see my husband over there," said Etienne. "I'll leave you two on your own. In a while."

"In a while," said Gallium and Legend.

King Dubian lay in bed, waiting for his wife to appear from the bath chamber. He stilled. There she stood before him, in a seductive, form-fitting gown with a low-cut bodice. Her firm thighs peeked out from the slits on each side.

"You look...incredible," he said.

She whirled around so he could get a look at the gown. "One of my best seamstresses made it for me! Isn't it perfect?"

Intoxicated by her beauty, he sat up on the side of the bed. "Not as perfect as you."

She sat down next to him and flicked a button on his uniform. "What's this? Why are you fully clothed?"

He sheepishly rubbed his head. "Well, I..."

She raised an eyebrow. "You what? Surely you don't think you'll copulate with me in your military uniform?"

"Well, you see... My—my body isn't as perfect as yours," he stammered. "I don't want you to find me lacking—especially not tonight."

She raised a brow. "Tonight is our wedding night. Now isn't the time to embrace insecurities." Cupping his chin with her hand, she said, "I married you for your heart, Dubian. Let's not begin our new life together with negative energy. All right?"

His eyes searched her face, silently begging her to understand. In the end, he knew she'd have her way. Having her love and approval was his air and water. Thus, he could never deny her anything.

Sighing, he got up and undressed in front of her. Her shocked gasp made him quickly hang his head in shame. Her eyes filled with sorrow.

"Come here, Dubian," she whispered.

Avoiding her eyes, he carefully sat on the bed. Tentatively, she traced the numerous rows of hardened welts and deep pits that covered most of his body.

"Who did this to you?" she murmured. "How did you get all of these terrible scars?"

His eyes hardened. "Queen Zherta often had me beaten by the soldiers in front of her. I was four summers the first time it happened."

She cupped his face and kissed him. "Why? What in the galaxy would make her do something so evil?"

"Pride. She's not my real mother. She only took me in so people would say she was virtuous. But she isn't. She's vain and selfish. I was a daily reminder my father cheated on her with a commoner. She couldn't punish my mother—she died. So she took her rage out on me."

She reached up and pulled his head down to rest on her generous breasts. "So that's why you didn't send her an invitation to the wedding."

He nodded. "Yes. She was furious, but I didn't care. A part of me wanted her to come so she'd know she hasn't broken me. But I didn't want her to say or do anything that would embarrass me. She hates me and the feeling is mutual."

He lifted his head to look at her. "How can you love someone as ugly as me? Don't you wish I looked like Gallium?"

She blinked. "Gallium? What on Platirius does he have to do with anything?"

"The eyes of every WomanForm—married or not—were on him tonight. You can't tell me you don't think he's handsome."

She frowned. "I wouldn't know because these eyes—" she pointed to hers "—were on you all night. And you're not ugly! You're my husband, Dubian. I love you!" She wanted to shake some sense into him. "I don't want to ever hear you speak of yourself in such a depreciating way or compare yourself to other Beings. Do you understand?"

He nodded. "All right," he said resignedly. "If you don't mind, I'd like for the lights to be turned off please."

She placed a hand on her hip. "And miss seeing my beauty in the light? Are you mad, Dubian? We're not copulating with the lights off—not on this night or any!"

He took her under the lights as she wanted, making his love for her all the more sweeter. She kissed every inch of his flesh that was covered in old wounds, sending a peace into his heart he'd never known existed.

Nine months later, she held a beautiful female InfantForm in her arms. King Dubian stared down at her little face, enchanted by her beauty. The little princess reached out and grabbed his long finger.

"She's so beautiful," he said. "She's the most beautiful InfantForm I've ever seen."

"Of course she is," she said, smiling down at her. "She's ours, isn't she?" She peered at her closely. "She has my eyes. And my nose...and my dimples!"

"She's perfect," he said. He looked up at her. "So are you." They shared a deep kiss before turning back to their daughter. "What will we call her?"

"Her name is Princess Vivant Elizabeth Amorous. She'll be the Queen of Platirius one day."

He nodded. "A righteous queen—just like her MotherForm. Princess Vivant, we are so happy to meet you."

The tiny princess cooed when he kissed her soft cheek. Their little family was happy for many years while the kingdoms of Platirius and Coldarius flourished.

He was so in love with his queen, he was content in giving her anything she wanted—until the announcement of a second InfantForm unleashed dark, repressed memories.

Demons of the past and old customs he thought were dead and buried rose within him. He was convinced the new life inside her would destroy his family.

How do I tell her without her getting upset?

He took a deep breath. "Dellah, Dr. Barrios told me having another InfantForm would endanger your life."

He wrung his hands. "It's too risky to go through with the pregnancy. You must sweep it away."

She was sitting at his desk preparing a speech she'd give at a neighboring planet. Stopping the pen mid-stroke, she looked up at her husband. Her soft, deadly tone made him shiver. "What did you just say to me, Dubian?"

He swallowed tightly. "Darling...I can't lose you—you know that. We're the perfect family—everyone envies us. Don't you think we have enough ChildForms?"

She tossed the pen onto the desk. "You're asking me what I think? I think I didn't enter myself and make myself pregnant. That was your doing," she said archly. "What do you mean, sweep it away? Do you think our baby is dirt in the road to be disposed of?"

"Of course not, Dellah. I'm just asking you to be reasonable!"

She pushed back the chair but didn't stand. "And I'm asking you to have a backbone! For once! Who is Dr. Barrios to dictate what I do with my life? Is he The One? Does he have a way of looking into my future and telling me what will or won't happen to me?"

"He's not the only one with concerns. After our daughter was born, other physicians said we may never have another InfantForm. You said you were all right with that!"

"There is no 'we,' Dubian. Only one of us has the ability to bear InfantForms, and I clearly recall what I said. I said if it were the will of The One for us not to have another InfantForm, then

I'd abide by it. That's what I said. If you're going to quote me, please do it properly."

She stood from the desk. "I'm not going to harm my baby. It'll be born—and if you don't like it, you don't have to witness it! You fainted the first time anyway."

"Now, Dear, don't get upset!" he begged.

"Don't get upset? You tell me to get rid of our baby then tell me not to get upset? What's gotten into you?"

"I'm sorry," he said.

She nodded. "You most certainly are," she said coldly. "You are the sorriest Being I've ever laid eyes on!"

"I'm only trying to take care of you! Why can't you see that? Most husbands don't care if their wives live or die, but I do. You should be more grateful you have me."

She tugged at the fashionable corded belt around her waist and imagined wrapping it around his neck until he—

"Leave me. Right now. I have a speech to prepare. I already feel queasy in the mornings, but I think if I sit here and look at you any longer, I'll vomit all over it."

He took a step toward her, attempting to console her.

"I said get out!" she shouted. "Now! You miserable, mangy animal!"

The cleaning staff stopped to listen in the hallway. They'd never heard the queen yelling at him. In fact, in all the years of their marriage, they'd never heard her raise her voice.

He hung his head. He hated seeing her upset. "I'll return after you've calmed yourself."

She sat down and took up the pen again. "Don't hurry back."

She didn't look up until he left. She set the pen down and rubbed her eyes. It had been good not to tell him about the waves of pain and fainting spells she'd had. He was wrong. She was grateful—to the staff who were more loyal to her than him. They wouldn't tell him anything without her permission.

"That damned Dr. Barrios," she said through gritted teeth. "I'll need to set him straight."

She pressed a button on the desk.

"Yes, Queen Dellah?"

"Find Dr. Barrios and send him into my meeting chamber."

"Yes, Your Highness. I'll get right on it!"

I n less than five minutes, Dr. Barrios hurried into the palace and bowed before her.

She calmly assessed him for a few moments, causing beads of sweat to gather on his forehead. "I won't waste your time or mine, Dr. Barrios. Where do you get off telling my husband I'm going to die? Are you some higher power none of us know about? If so, please enlighten me. Maybe I should be bowing to you."

He nervously adjusted his collar. "Uh—oh no, Your Majesty! I have no authority at all!"

She narrowed her eyes and crossed her legs. "Then in the future, you'll keep your mouth shut concerning matters that don't concern you, yes?"

He bowed furiously. "Forgive me, Queen Dellah. I only told the king—"

"Things that weren't your business to tell," she concluded. She drummed her manicured nails on the desk. "Now let's talk about your business, shall we? Are Gallium or your parents aware of your little secret?"

He visibly paled before her.

"I thought not. Oh yes, I've known about you for quite some time but I haven't told anyone. I have a lot of respect for your parents—and Gallium. It would kill your family if they knew what you've become."

She pulled up his credentials on the TranScreen. "Not to mention your career would be ruined faster than the time it took to put Ana Weiss down like the rabid dog she was."

He lowered his head.

"Oh no. I'll have none of that. You've placed yourself in this position. At least be masculine enough to look me in the eye!"

She waited until he made eye contact. "That's better. Let me be very clear. If you stick your nose in my business again, I'll broadcast yours from here to Platz. I haven't dealt with you because I don't want to hurt Gallium."

He watched as she tightly wrapped her belt around her fist. "But make no mistake, if you cross me again, I'll cut you down right in front of him. Have I been heard?"

"Yes, Your Highness," he whispered.

"I can't hear you, Dr. Barrios."

"Yes, Queen Dellah," he said.

"Good. I'm glad we could reach an understanding. I'm sure you're very busy, Doctor. I won't keep you."

"Thank you, Queen Dellah!"

Chuckling to herself, she watched him scamper off like a scared rabbit. "What a waste," she said softly. "On the surface, one would never know he and Gallium were brothers."

Her baby kicked within her. Lovingly, she placed a hand on her belly. "Don't you worry, little one. Your father is afraid of you, but I won't allow him to treat you the way King Anemi treated him. None of their generational curses will affect you or your sister. You have my word on that."

A small bell went off. The surveillance chamber was dispatching her.

"Yes, what is it, General Iham?"

"There's something I think you should know, My Queen. King Dubian is discussing your personal business with General Sodom."

Her beautiful silver eyes narrowed. "Send the footage to my TranScreen."

General Iham saluted her. "Yes, Your Highness."

I n five minutes, her petite hand smacked open the door. King Dubian was sitting with his head in his hands.

"What am I going to do, General Sodom? I never wanted a second ChildForm but she's determined to risk her health having it!"

"How dare you sit in here and discuss our business with him!" she shouted. "Are you married to him or I? Where does your loyalty lie, you slimy snake?"

General Sodom looked as if he'd rather be anywhere but there.

King Dubian jumped out of the chair. "I'm loyal to you!" he whined. "You know that!"

"What I know is you're running to tattle to General Sodom as if he's a teacher who'll paddle my bottom! A servant in my army! I don't see him running to you to talk about his wife! Where is your backbone?"

"If you'll excuse me, Your Majesties," said General Sodom.

She pounced on him like an eagle on a mouse. "Did I say you could leave, General?"

He stopped mid-step, his eyes wider than space. Watching from the comfort of the surveillance chamber, General Iham chuckled. He never missed an opportunity to see the insufferable General Sodom humbled.

Her stare pinned him in place. "Since you're in such a hurry to leave, I suggest you prepare to go to Kikhani. It seems King Hitam has grown overly confident in his abilities and believes he's fit enough to take over Platirius. He should be reminded of precisely who he's dealing with."

He saluted her. "Yes, Queen Dellah. I'll prepare our troops right now!"

"And General Sodom? The only way you'd better return to Platirius is victorious or dead. Have I been heard?"

General Iham covered his mouth to keep from laughing out loud. General Sodom didn't dare look at King Dubian. The true power behind Platirius's military was staring him in the face.

"Yes, My Queen. I understand! Platirius will be victorious against Kikhani!"

She nodded. "That's what I want to hear, Sodom. Now get going."

He hurried out of his office as she turned to look at her husband. The door closed slowly behind her.

After the tongue lashing he'd received, King Dubian sought to take his anger out on someone. He found a source—Gallium. In a huff, he entered the gardening chamber and began throwing things around.

Gallium jumped up. "King Dubian! Those are dangerous substances! I wouldn't rattle them."

It was too late. Vials of powder exploded against the wall, releasing a stream of gasses, causing him to cough and fall to the floor. Gallium pushed the alarm and fell to the floor with a satisfied grin.

A soldier rushed inside the palace to find her. "My Queen, King Dubian went into the gardening chamber where Gallium was working and started tossing the substances you ordered him to make to kill the Kikhanians! The king and Gallium have been rushed to the medical chamber!"

She pushed aside the slice of peach pie she'd dug into. "No! That idiot! By The One, what was he thinking? Are they dead?"

"No, Your Highness! But both are knocked out cold!"

She ran as fast as her extended belly would allow. Finally reaching the medical chamber, she glanced down at her husband. Swiftly passing him by, she went to Gallium's side and took his hand.

Peering into his face, she asked, "Dr. Barrios, is he going to be all right?"

"I've run some tests but the results haven't come back yet. I expect King Dubian to awaken shortly."

She glared up at him. "I want you to take a good look at whose hand I'm holding. Does that give you a clue as to who I'm asking about?"

He removed his glasses and rubbed his eyes. "Er—well...the gases King Dubian released are very harmful. I'm happy to report they didn't suffer serious injuries, but I need to test Gallium further to find out why he's still asleep."

"Ohhh," said King Dubian. "My head!" He sat up on the padded table.

She narrowed her eyes. "If Gallium dies, your head won't be the only thing that hurts. Do you ever think of anyone but yourself? The King of Platirius throwing a tantrum like a small ChildForm! You could have killed him! Don't you know not to trifle with chemicals you don't understand?"

He sat looking like a lost puppy. Meanwhile, Gallium opened one eye and winked at Dr. Barrios, who struggled to hide his surprise.

She nodded at a group of soldiers guarding the medical chamber. "Get him out of my sight. Take him back to the palace."

The soldiers saluted her. "Yes, Queen Dellah!"

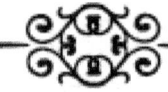

K

ing Dubian allowed himself to be escorted out of the medical chamber, but just before they reached the palace stairs, he said, "Take your dirty hands off me!"

Immediately, he was released. The soldiers watched him ascend the stairs in veiled distaste.

Corporal Azini muttered, "His own wife cares more about Gallium than him. How humiliating."

Corporal Badghetz said, "It serves him right for being so weak. She'll always care about Coldarians more than him. If he dies, I hope she marries one of us and makes him the next king."

Corporal Azini nodded. "Let's hope he dies quickly."

He started to spit on the palace steps but checked himself. Queen Dellah lived there too. Since she had the absolute loyalty of the military, they'd never disrespect her.

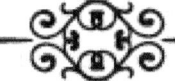

She turned to Dr. Barrios. "I want to be informed the minute he wakes up. Not a second longer!"

He bowed to her. "Yes, Queen Dellah. I'll make sure you're notified immediately."

She looked down at Gallium once more before turning on her heel. Her husband was acting like a rabid animal that needed to be put out of its misery. Little did he know, she was the perfect one to do it. Dr. Barrios waited until she was out of sight before he focused his attention on Gallium.

"Are you crazy? Why are you pretending to be hurt when you're not? And how are you not hurt? Those gases should've killed you!"

Gallium smiled and extended his hand. Dr. Barrios grabbed it and pulled him up. "You're wrong, Doctor. Gases or anything made from plants have no effect on me."

Dr. Barrios grabbed his shoulders. "What do you mean?"

Gallium looked him in the eye. "I mean I can't die. No matter what the substance is—no matter where it's made—it won't kill me. I am impervious to the weapons I make."

Dr. Barrios took off his glasses and wiped his eyes. It had been a long night. "How is that possible?"

"I don't know," admitted Gallium. "But it's true. Not only is my body invincible, I can control plants with my mind."

"Explain this to me, Gallium."

"When I touch plants—especially anything poisonous—I can extract the poison just by thinking it. I can also make anything I conjure up. Take jewels and flowers—I can change the molecular structure with just a touch and my imagination. That's how I was able to make the diamond roses."

He sat still as a group of wires were pulled from his chest. "Plants listen to me and I hear them. They speak to me, Ezra. They tell me I'm their master. That's why they don't harm me. I discovered my gift when I was in my twelfth summer."

Dr. Barrios ran his hands through his hair. "And you never told anyone—not me or Mother or Father?"

"How could I tell you? I don't know how, why, or when I received the gift. All I know is...it's there." He laughed. "That was a ride to lay there and act like I was hurt. I knew King Dubian would get it, and if I know the queen, she's tearing him apart right now!"

Dr. Barrios groaned. "Queen Dellah! I'd better inform her you're up and about." He pointed at Gallium. "If I were you, I wouldn't keep this from her! She cares about you. Trust me, you don't want to get on her bad side."

Gallium swung his legs over the side of the table. "I will...once I see how she punishes King Dubian. He's had it coming for quite a while."

"By The One... My brother is... I don't even know how to describe you. I need to run more tests to see if I can discover what happened to you."

Gallium was still looking in the direction Queen Dellah had departed. "Run all the tests you'd like. It won't change anything." He closed his hand into a fist. "Platirius's king is about to discover a different kind of power in good time."

He and Dr. Barrios smiled at each other.

She turned her back on him when they lay down to sleep and got up the next morning without greeting him. He'd never felt so alone. He was pleased when she summoned him to the meeting chamber.

"My Queen, please allow me to apologize for what happened yesterday."

She raised her hand. "There's no need for that. Sit down, Dubian."

She ignored his outstretched hand. The WomanForm he loved looked over him as if she were sizing him up to send him into battle.

"I'd like for you to clear something up for me. Did you read any of the documents you signed before Coldarius merged with Platirius?"

He sat up straight, clearly confused by her question. "No, I didn't. I knew you drafted the stipulations for the merger, so there was no need. You know I'll abide by anything you want, Dellah."

She nodded. "Well, that's good. But I'd like for you to take a look at this one."

She raised her palm, patiently allowing him to read the fine print on the form. His lips tightened. He hadn't realized just how ruthless she could be.

Instead of being annoyed by her aloofness, he found it to be quite tantalizing. When she rebuked, ignored, or dismissed him, it only made him want her more. He realized he needed her approval more than he needed oxygen in his lungs.

"I am a Coldarian, first and foremost. So it shouldn't surprise you that I'd place the well-being of Coldarians over Platirians.

One of my stipulations was that Platirians never try and harm Coldarians—at least not without consequences."

She raised her eyes to meet his before continuing. "You have no idea what Gallium is capable of, but my father and I do. Long before I hired him, I made a mental note to draft a special clause into the merger contract specifically for him."

His smile tightened. He never would've guessed she'd been thinking of Gallium before they married. Had she— No. He refused to think it.

"He's much more valuable to us than you could ever imagine. Now, you're aware the chemicals he makes are deadly to our enemies. If he were to be taken by another planet, his talents could be used against us. That makes him the most important Coldarian on Platirius."

She got up and poured a drink for him. "If you knew how much money he's brought in, it would make your greedy father roll over and sit up in his grave. But his significance goes even further than that. No matter who we go to war with, we will win as long as Gallium fights with us."

She set the drink before him. "He has a special ability—I think he was born with it. He learned about it during his transition period from ChildForm to MaleForm, but we've always known. That's why Father and I wanted him."

He leaned forward when she sat in front of him. Despite hating hearing about Gallium, the scent of her perfume was intoxicating.

"What I'm saying is Gallium is more important to Platirius than you. You're not a soldier. You can't win a fist fight nor do you know how to command an army. So, I'll make this clear: If you raise a hand to him again, either in my presence or long after I'm dead, you'll be immediately dethroned as king."

"Dellah!"

Her voice rose over his. "And Gallium will be the next King of Platirius!" She raised her palm again. "You agreed to it. This is your signature, yes?"

He downed the drink and looked out a window.

"My father specifically asked if you were reading the documents before you signed them. There was a good reason for that. But you didn't."

She leaned back and folded her hands over her belly. "Now? There's no going back. I'm set to control the greatest empires in the universe. I refuse to allow weakness to interfere with my plans. I wasn't going to make this public, but you've left me with no choice. Taking Gallium's head is off-limits. To everyone."

He hung his head.

"That includes you, my dear husband," she said softly. "If you get in my way, I won't hesitate to throw you into the Flames of Justice."

She rose to her feet, looking down on him. "So, if I were you, I'd get on board with my vision and do it quickly. I didn't come to Platirius for Coldarius to be left on the sidelines. I came to advance my planet—over yours."

She lifted his head when he would've hung it. "And I've done it. You've given me free reign to do so, but it cannot be undone. I own the military and every head in every chamber in both kingdoms."

She paused to refill his drink. "I've earned their trust by treating them with compassion while you've spit on everyone except myself and my father. You're welcome to try and gather a coup to overthrow me, but I assure you, no one will betray me for you."

His fingers toyed with the beads on her gown. "That won't be necessary. I don't want anything to change. You're my wife—I love you. I don't know how to make you understand that."

"By showing obedience and loyalty. Loyalty to our family—including the new baby—and to my reign as queen."

He raised the glass to her. "You have it. I give you my respect, love, and loyalty. Always."

She nodded solemnly. "Good. I'm glad that's over. I don't like it when we fight."

"Neither do I," he said tightly.

She extended her hand. "Come, let's see what the dining chamber has to offer. I'm hungry."

He reached for her hand, kissing it soundly. Everything would be all right. As long as she was in charge, Platirius would continue to thrive. He'd die before he allowed a lowly gardener to take his place in her heart—and his bed. Everyone paused to bow as the King and Queen of Platirius descended the palace stairs.

It was clear to everyone that she'd succeeded in getting her way. Again. The Platirians were relieved—especially the WomenForms. Under her rule, they were spared from her husband's childish antics. Everyone wished her a long life filled with prosperity.

Everyone...except one.

Chapter 4

"My King, Lady Alarah has arrived to see you."

King Carlomon looked up from reading and glanced briefly at the soldier before nodding. "Send her in."

She breezed past the soldier and bowed to him.

"Hello, Lady Alarah. I must say…this is a surprise. My condolences on the loss of your son. I didn't expect to see you up and about so soon. How are you feeling?"

She unwrapped her expensive shawl from around her neck. "I feel fine, Your Highness. Things happen, but I can't spend my life locked away grieving. It was a disappointment, but so is my marriage. She tossed a sultry look his way. "He could've been yours, had you forgiven me."

He sighed and looked out at the falling snow.

What kind of WomanForm doesn't grieve over the loss of her InfantForm?

He imagined how devastated his wife would've been had she lost a son.

"I see you're still stuck on your version of the past. Did you forget you left me as soon as you learned half of my leg had been blown off in battle? You didn't respect me enough to wait until I was released from the medical chamber before you married General Iham."

He raised his hand to stop her. "I have nothing but good things to say about him. He's a good MaleForm and an excellent commander. I've never held it against you, so there's really no need to bring up the past."

Her grip tightened on the shawl. "You make it seem as if I abandoned you."

"There's no gray area. I said it plainly. Thank you for calling it what it was—abandonment."

"I didn't know if you'd return from Ziltach dead or alive. The only news we heard was that none of our soldiers made it out alive. What other choice did I have?"

He looked at her dispassionately. She spun lies as easily as a spider spinning a web. Truthfully, he was glad she'd dumped him for General Iham. He hadn't realized how selfish and ambitious she was in their youth.

He silently thanked The One for sending his wife into his life while he was in the throes of despair. She'd helped to heal his body and his mind. Together, they had ruled Coldarius on love and compassion—things Lady Alarah knew nothing about.

She laid the shawl on the arm of a leather chair. "Before I could blink, you were engaged to Elia and wanted to make her your queen. I tried convincing you not to throw away our love, but you wouldn't listen."

His half-smile held no warmth. "No, you tried to manipulate me into coming back to you so that you'd be queen instead of her. No one expected my brother to die, but the throne passed to me when he did. Had I remained second in command of Coldarius, I would've still been nothing more to you than useless baggage."

Her eye twitched. "You misunderstood my words."

"My leg was damaged in battle, not my brain. I overheard you speaking with your snooty friends quite clearly. And trust me, I understood your meaning loud and clear. It was the power you wanted, never me."

She rolled her eyes, unconsciously focusing on the highly polished bookcases. The custom-made, floor-to-ceiling shelves were built from the finest materials. The extraordinary library had been a birthday present from Queen Elia during the first year of their marriage.

They'd spent many hours together, reading and discussing their favorite scenes and dialogue. Not a day passed he hadn't wished she were still with him.

"You're still so stubborn." Her fingertip lightly touched the spine of one of the damask-covered books. "And still in love with your boring books."

He reached for his cane. It was time for her to leave. "And what of you? You have a devoted husband and a beautiful daughter. What do you love? Other than yourself, that is?"

"King Carlomon—"

His hard tone cut her short. "It's so cold outside, not a single animal is roaming around. Yet, here you stand spouting nonsense. What possessed you to come to me on a night like this?"

"General Iham is still on Platirius and our daughter is with a NurseForm."

He frowned at her. "Oh? And what does that have to do with me?"

She moistened her lips. "Your wife has been dead for years. It makes no sense for you to stay locked away in this palace, waiting to join her. You're still young. We can start over again if only you'd allow it."

Balancing his weight on the cane, he stood. "WomanForm, are you out of your mind? You're married to one of the finest soldiers I've ever had. You've just lost his InfantForm, but he's willing to try to have another. Are you never satisfied with the blessings of The One?"

She bristled. "I lost it because I wanted to—it wasn't by accident!"

Repulsed, he stepped back from her. He'd never pitied General Iham more than he did now.

"I heard my husband is to be dispatched to Kikhani. They've declared war on Platirius."

He expanded his hands. "And? Are you hoping he'll be killed in battle?"

To his horror, she nodded. "That would pave the way for us to be together, wouldn't it? My daughter would be raised in a palace the way your daughter was. Queen Dellah lives in palace grander than this and is loved by everyone. But we don't have to wait until he dies."

She took a step toward him and placed her hands on his strong chest. "We could be together now. I still know how to make you moan."

He shoved her away. Rubbing a hand through his hair, he gazed at her, almost frightened by what he saw. "You are...amoral. Your heart is blacker than King Anemi's. If you think I'd lower myself to carry on with a married WomanForm, then you never knew me."

Her pretty face hardened. "Oh? Because your precious queen was perfect, right? The gall of you to choose a broken WomanForm over me!"

"Broken? My Elia was more whole than you'll ever be—in body, mind, and spirit! You sound like a disgusting ableist. I'll hear no more of your prejudices against Beings with impairments—including myself!"

His lip curled in distaste. "Get this through your warped skull—we're *not* beneath Beings without visible disabilities. Elia helped me to see that. Marrying you would've kept my self-esteem in the gutter. I thank The One for sending my wife when I needed her the most. You spread toxicity like a virus."

Backing away from her as if she were contagious, he said, "You poison everything you touch, Alarah."

Blinded by rage, she lunged forward and tried to knock his cane out of his hand.

"And your daughter? Is she the pillar of righteousness? Her weak-minded husband practically trips over her every move! Anyone who disagrees with her gets killed! No one on Platirius has received a proper burial since she became queen. What she did to Ana Weiss and her family was abominable!"

His hollow chuckle filled the study. "I'm not surprised you and Ana Weiss were friends. Ana shredded reputations like cloth—there's the real atrocity. I don't see anyone complaining she's gone."

She took a step forward. "That's because no one is crazy enough to challenge her! They're afraid they'll be murdered too!"

He tried to summon an ounce of pity for her, but it was difficult. "What are you afraid of? Does anything keep you up at night?"

Her haughty blue-green eyes flashed like fire. "I fear living a life of mediocrity and dying before I get all that I deserve. I've had to fight and claw my way to the top, unlike your spoiled, selfish daughter! She had no right to force her opinions on Ana!"

She'd finally struck a nerve. "My daughter laid down the rules, but Ana thought she could spit on them. She earned what she got!"

"And what about you, My King? What will you earn when you finally get what's coming to you?!" she shouted.

His eyes traveled over her in disgust. "I'm not your husband. I'll remind you once to remember where you are and to whom you're speaking. You're just as unbalanced as ever, but I don't fear it, nor am I impressed by it."

He returned the book to its place. After listening to her antics, he wasn't in the mood to read. "You've always been jealous of any WomanForm you felt was more successful than you. I don't know what I ever saw in you, but I'm going to try extremely hard not to remember that I ever had feelings for you."

He turned his back to her. "You've stated your peace, now leave and never return."

She grabbed his elbow. "If I were you, I wouldn't turn me away."

He snatched away from her. "And if I were you, I wouldn't threaten me. I'm not as twisted as King Anemi, but don't think I'll stand here and let you be insolent to my face! It would be unfortunate for your daughter, but I won't hesitate to throw you in my confinement chamber!"

"Now that's the strong king I know and admire," she purred.

He stepped around her with the agility of a cat. Lifting her shawl from the chair, he flung it at her. "Save your weak flattery for someone dumb enough to fall for it. We're finished here. Don't make me tell you again to leave."

She stood silently, not daring to voice the threat standing in her eyes. Clutching the shawl in a death grip, she stormed out.

A soldier came rushing in. "I heard raised voices. Are you all right, My King?"

He sighed. "I'm fine. Inform all the guards that WomanForm is never allowed through my gates again."

The soldier saluted him. "Yes, My King. I'll spread the word."

Lady Alarah stood outside in the cold, looking up at the light in the library's window. "You think you're so high and mighty, but I'll make you regret rejecting me. When I'm finished with you and your spoiled, pampered daughter, I swear by The One, you'll wish you'd embraced me!"

Wrapping her shawl around her neck, she walked onto the road and disappeared into the night.

Gallium sat with Queen Dellah in one of the royal gardens. "Are you sure you're alright, Gallium?"

"I'm fine, My Queen, but there's something I have to tell you. If you want to punish me, I'll understand." His eyes searched hers. "I wasn't hurt in the gardening chamber. I only laid low so King Dubian could get into trouble."

Her warm, silver eyes were unreadable. "Go on," she said.

He tugged on his hair. "The chemicals I made didn't hurt me. None of them do."

The corners of her mouth curled upward, and all of a sudden...he knew.

"You've known about me all along, haven't you?"

She nodded. "When you were a baby, maybe in your second summer? You ate some ChantaBobs. My father had you rushed to the medical chamber. The poison should've killed you, but it didn't. Our medical staff were amazed they made you stronger. After that, you thrived. My mother and I became very attached to you."

She motioned for him to turn around so she could tighten the strip of leather that had loosened in his hair. "My father asked your parents if you could stay with us a bit longer. He asked the research staff to monitor you for another year and study your ability to manipulate plants. But they never discovered how you did it."

She smiled at him. "Since you couldn't speak yet, you couldn't tell us either. Oh, you were the cutest baby—tons of curly black hair, plump cheeks, and the most adorable sea-green eyes. I see you're still charming WomenForms across Space with those eyes."

He blushed and looked away. No matter how many compliments he received, he'd never turned arrogant. "Once he understood a bit of what you could do, my father sent you home. But he didn't tell your parents what he'd learned. He wanted to see how you'd respond to your natural environment."

She finished tying the strip and sat back to scrutinize her work. "We've kept tabs on you all these years."

"That's why you hired me," he said quietly.

"That's one of the reasons," she admitted. "The other was I grew quite fond of having a brother. It broke my heart when you returned to your family. My mother's too. I've been blessed to watch you grow and to form a genuine friendship with you."

She reached over and squeezed his hand. "Never think you're just a servant to me. I truly believe you are a blessing bestowed on us by The One. There's no one like you, Gallium, and I'm so proud to call you my friend."

He ducked to hide the tears in his eyes. "Thank you, Queen Dellah."

She reached down and plucked a violet to place in her hair. "You're welcome. My husband is aware if he lifts a finger in anger toward you again, you'll take his place as king."

Speechless, he gawked at her.

"I mean every word. Coldarius will be on top—even if it comes at Platirius's expense. It would be nothing for me to cut off his head and absorb Platirius into Coldarius. I hate to admit it, but I think most of our subjects would be happier with him gone." She turned to him. "And you'd make it happen with me. Dubian is fully aware I'm not one to toy with."

He smiled. "I agree, Your Highness. You are fearless!"

"Mmhmm. And I think," she said, patting her stomach, "this one will be too!"

He eyed her round belly. "Do you think it will be female?"

She smiled happily. "Oh yes. I feel it in my soul."

"Mother!" Princess Vivant came running over to them.

"Yes, my little puppy? Mind your manners and say hello to Gallium."

She looked at him shyly, biting on her nail.

"Don't bite your nails, Vivant. A lady's hands must always be smooth and beautiful."

Immediately, she removed her finger from her mouth. Impatiently, she bounced from foot to foot.

Queen Dellah leaned over to adjust a ribbon on her sock. "What is it, my sweet daughter?"

"Mother, may I have lavender butter toffee cookies for lunch?"

Her lips pursed. "You mean after lunch?"

Exasperated, the ChildForm shook her head. "No. I only want cookies for lunch!"

She sucked her teeth. "Absolutely not. You may have a couple cookies after lunch, but not as a substitute for your meal."

The princess pouted, but she knew better than to disobey her. "Okay," she said sadly.

Queen Dellah and Gallium hid their smiles.

"Is that all you needed from me?"

"Yes, the dining staff just finished baking them. Don't they smell wonderful, Mother? We could share them."

Her mother smiled at her precocious attempt to persuade her. "Yes, they do, and yes, we could, but that won't change my mind."

She gave up and placed her hands on her mother's belly and kissed it. "I'm going to share my cookies with my baby sister when she comes!" she promised.

"That's very sweet of you," said Queen Dellah, lifting her hand and placing a soft kiss on it.

"Bye bye, baby sister! I'll be back to read you a story!" She ran off, leaving them laughing at her small, retreating form.

"Her innocence is so refreshing," she said. "I hope that never changes."

"With you as her MotherForm, it won't. I'm confident you'll rear both of your daughters to be just as excellent as you are, Your Highness."

Filled with pride, she watched her skip into the royal dining chamber. "High words of praise, my friend. I thank you."

"Thank you for not treating me like an outcast, but I'm not ready for anyone to know I'm different. Is that all right?"

She punched him in his shoulder. "I would never do that! You call it different, but I say you're gifted. You should be proud of your abilities, not repulsed by them."

He looked off into the distance.

She gently patted his forearm. "All right. You win. I'll keep your secret. Dubian knows, but he won't breathe a word. He's too afraid someone might ask you to end him."

Lifting his eyebrows, he turned to her. "End him, huh? And who would that someone be?" He chuckled at her sly wink. "Intellect and beauty is a dangerous combination."

She smirked. "Don't I know it," she said smugly.

A dining staff appeared and bowed before her. "My Queen, I'm sorry to interrupt you." She bit her lip nervously. "Princess Vivant said she could have cookies before lunch. I wouldn't dare ask, but we got into a bit of trouble with King Dubian the last time we gave her sweets before a meal."

Gallium assisted a very pregnant Queen Dellah to her feet. "Princess Vivant!" she called, waddling toward the palace's dining chamber.

L egend had just finished putting away the last of the inventory when the bell above the door chimed.

She held her breath. *Could it be him?*

It had been nearly a year since she had seen Gallium. Although they sent frequent messages by TeleScreen, it wasn't enough. She missed him.

There were so many things she wished she had said to him before he left. Now she feared it would be too late. She doubted King Dubian had lifted a finger to review her application. General Iham told her no WomenForms currently served under him.

Queen Dellah approved of them joining, but she wanted to ensure she would oversee their training and safety. As quietly as it was kept, her second pregnancy had been difficult. On many occasions, she was too ill to leave her bed chamber. But Legend wasn't worried about her.

The queen was as strong and fierce as any of them. She just had to be patient and wait until the new InfantForm arrived. Then she'd re-apply.

She turned to assist the customer. The warm greeting died on her lips instantly.

What on Coldarius is she doing here?

Lady Alarah looked around the shop as if she expected TophoBugs to slither from under the counter. She forced herself to keep her tone professional.

Being the wife of General Iham provided a lot of influence that she never missed an opportunity to wield to her advantage. She was an evil, nasty WomanForm whom no one liked. Even her alleged friends gossiped about her behind her back.

Legend heard her best friend, Ana Weiss, had been executed. While she didn't feel sorry for her, she knew her mother couldn't afford any bad-mouthing of her business. She believed Lady Alarah awakened to drink misery for energy.

She smiled warmly at the older WomanForm. "Welcome, Lady Alarah. How may I help you?"

"For starters, you can fetch a dozen of those blue roses Gallium grew for Queen Dellah's wedding. Nothing in here looks even close to being that impressive."

She allowed the insult roll off her back. If Lady Alarah wanted to carry around dozens of life's bricks, that was her business. She wouldn't allow her to drop them at her feet.

"We don't have those in stock. I would have to place a special order for Gallium to design them for you."

She scowled. "And how long will that take? I shouldn't have to wait. You should have them available!"

Legend held on to her patience. "We've never had blue roses. They were custom made for Queen Dellah. I'm not even sure if he has time to make them for you."

She swiped her finger on the counter, checking for dust. "What exactly *are* you sure of, Legend? How do you call yourself a business owner when you don't have what customers need?"

Legend decided it wasn't worth engaging with her. She turned and picked up some ledgers. "I'll send a message to Gallium and ask him about the roses. Is there anything else you'll need?"

She wasn't used to being dismissed. "As a matter of fact, there is. Tell him I want three dozen of those diamond roses he grew for her too."

Legend scanned her request on her palm. "And a dozen of the blue ones?"

"On second thought, I'll take three dozen of those too. Be sure to inform me when they're ready." She turned to leave without waiting for a response.

Legend shook her head. "She's so sure she'll get what she wants," she muttered.

It didn't take long for Gallium to respond.

"You know I'd do anything for you, but I'm not arranging anything for her. She was rude to my mother at the wedding. Second, Queen Dellah won't approve of her roses being re-created just for her. She can't stand the ground Lady Alarah walks on. If you want, I'll ask the queen to send word to her so she won't take it out on you and Mrs. Guilde."

She smiled at the note. "Thank you!" she wrote back. "Your mother is one of the kindest Beings I know. The way Lady Alarah treats others is inexcusable. Nothing will give me more pleasure than seeing the look on her face when she finds out she can't have the roses!"

Sure enough, she breezed into the flower shop the next day. "I'd like a dozen red roses and a dozen white, please," she said in a hushed tone.

Legend observed her quiet demeanor. In all the time she'd known her, she'd never heard her say please or thank you. That made her smile. "Of course, Lady Alarah. I'll get them ready for you right now."

She silently watched her wrap the roses in the prettiest paper she could find. The luxurious different shades of blue created a dramatic effect against the hues of the flowers. Legend raised her palm to accept the payment.

Lady Alarah made the payment, collected the roses, and started toward the door before she turned around to face Legend. "Thank you," she said stiffly.

It took all of Legend's strength not to laugh. "You're welcome, Lady Alarah. Please visit us again soon."

She left without another word. Gallium had sent a second note to Legend before she opened the shop. "*Not only did Queen Dellah deny her request, she told her if she so much as breathed on you wrong, she'd be summoned to Platirius for a meeting with her. I doubt she'll give you any more problems.*"

Before the work day was over, she opened her TeleScreen to receive another transmission.

Queen Dellah's beautiful face appeared on the screen. "Hello, Legend. Did Lady Alarah visit the shop today?"

"Hello, Your Highness. Yes, she did, but she didn't give me any problems. In fact, she acted like a genuine lady."

Queen Dellah harrumphed. "I've been waiting a long time for her to cross me. Let me know if she gives you the slightest issue. Trust me, I'll take care of her."

Legend bowed gracefully. "Thank you, Queen Dellah. I can't express how much that means to us."

She nodded and smiled. "You're more than welcome, Legend. Any friend of Gallium is a friend of mine. And don't worry, I know you want to join Platirius's army. I have you and a few other WomenForms in mind. I'll handle everything after my baby comes. In a while."

"Thank you again. In a while, My Queen."

*S*he wants Gallium. Not you!

King Dubian's head was pounding. The strange voices had tormented him since before dawn. The harder he tried to ignore them, the more incessant they became.

The baby belongs to Gallium. That's why she wants to keep it. If it were yours, she would've passed it from her body by now.

"That's not true!" he said. "She would never betray me!"

Oh, but she would! She's a Coldarian. She's placed her race above yours—above all Platirians. What kind of king allows a WomanForm to muzzle him like a dog? You're weak, Dubian! You've always been weak! That's why you murdered me in my bed—so I wouldn't remind you of how worthless you are!

"Get out of my head!" he shouted. He gritted his teeth. Quozinite! It would help him sleep. He'd been working too hard to make things work with the Coldarians, but taking Quozinite would help him feel better.

Ignoring the curious stares that followed him to his bed chamber, he found it tucked away in a drawer in his wardrobe. His hands shook as he tried to open the crystal bottle.

That's right, fool. Take the substance Gallium made. They're trying to poison you, you know? And once you're dead, he'll take your place. He'll sit on your throne—on top of your wife! You're allowing it by taking the poison he fashioned to kill you! Idiot!

He poured a glass of wine and downed two small packets in one gulp. It wasn't long before he felt woozy. He sat on the edge of the bed before leaning back and getting lost in the softness of the bedding.

He walked down a long hallway alone. The palace was empty except for strange sounds coming from the end of the corridor. He kept walking until he reached a door. Putting his ear up to it, he heard soft moans coming from the other side. Gently, he pushed open the door and saw—Dellah! His Dellah was in Gallium's arms!

They were copulating in his bed! He unsheathed his dagger and crept closer to them. They were so engaged that they didn't hear him advancing toward them. She mounted Gallium and threw her head back, moaning in ecstasy. Suddenly, she opened her eyes and screamed.

The blade sliced at her throat, ripping through the delicate skin and tissue. He watched her fall at Gallium's side. The lowly gardener was laughing at him! He raised his arm to strike him down, but it wouldn't move!

Gallium, still laughing, trained his attention on a row of vines growing along the wall. They lashed out, encircling his throat—strangling him.

The dagger fell from his hand as he struggled to free himself from their unyielding grip. They pulled tighter against his throat, causing him to sink to his knees. He was going to die! Gallium stood over him, his mocking laughter ringing in the air. Queen Dellah raised from the bed and stood at his side.

He stared in horror at the blood running from her neck. Gallium said, "Everything you have is mine now. No one will remember your name." The lovers embraced each other. He floated high above their heads. Space parted where a door opened to a blazing inferno of flames hungrily licking for his flesh.

"Noooooooooooo!" he screamed.

"Dubian!" Queen Dellah came rushing into the bed chamber, followed by two soldiers. "What is it? What's wrong?"

He wiped a hand over his face. "Dellah—I—"

She kneeled on the bed, gathering his face in her hands. "Are you hurt?"

He shook his head. "No! I had a nightmare." Breathing heavily, he met her worried eyes.

She rubbed her hands down his arms. "Everything is alright now. It was just a dream. You're safe. Whatever it was, it's not real."

He shuddered.

"Look at me," she said. "It's over. Nothing is going to hurt you. Do you understand?"

He swallowed hard and nodded. "Yes, I understand."

She wiped the sweat from his brow before looking over her shoulder to the soldiers. "You may leave us. The king is fine."

The soldiers saluted her. She turned back and scanned his face. "Handling the merger has taken a lot out of you, hasn't it? I'm sorry you had to take on the burden of my responsibilities. Maybe we should postpone the trip to Maieman so you can rest?"

"No. We've made promises to the king and queen. We've lost too many soldiers—we have to replenish our ranks." He rubbed a hand over his eyes.

"We can't allow the Kikhanians to overpower us. Maieman is the closest planet to us and their military is first-rate. King Micah has been a long-time ally to us and Kikhani. If we don't attend, they may be inclined to side with King Hitam."

He caressed her shoulders. "We need them, Dellah. We must defeat him."

She placed her hand on top of his. "We will. He's a skilled warrior, but it's Kikhani against Platirius *and* Coldarius. Even he can't defeat two planets."

He looked into the distance. "I still want the Maieman soldiers. If we're going to make our military invincible, we'll need only the best."

She sighed and sat beside him. "All right, but only if you're sure you're well enough to go. The gala is tomorrow evening. We'll have to fly out early to get there on time."

He grabbed her hand and kissed it. "Is your new gown ready?"

"Of course. I'm all packed and ready to go. You'll need to instruct the staff to pack your personal items and we're all set. They've already packed up your wardrobe."

She'll leave you on Maieman to die!

A clouded look came into his eyes.

Her brow furrowed. "Dubian? What's the matter?"

"Nothing. I'll be ready to go in the morning." He gave her a weak smile. "Are you hungry? I've been craving some beef bone soup and a few of those excellent rolls you gave our dining staff the recipe for."

She scooted off the bed. "I'll send up the order and have our supper brought here. Just sit back and I'll take care of everything."

He rubbed her thigh. "You always do. You take such good care of me."

She planted a kiss on his forehead. "And I always will. Someone has to make up for that wretched Queen Zherta failing to care for you properly."

At the mention of Queen Zherta, he stiffened.

"She's gone, Dubian," she said, stroking his back. "She'll never hurt you again. Not as long as I'm alive."

"I'm going to hold you to that. You're not allowed to die. Not ever."

She gave him a mock salute. "Yes, My King! I have my orders to stay alive!"

It pleased him to hear her laughing again. It had been a long time since she'd enjoyed his company. He was grateful things seemed to be shifting back to normal.

"Now," she said, pointing to the bed. "Get comfortable and find something entertaining on the TranScreen. The surveillance staff told me the Humans are protesting another war. That should be a hoot!"

"Ah, the Humans. They are nothing if not entertaining, hm?"

She sniffed. "They most certainly are. Try and relax. I'll be back shortly."

"Thank you, Dellah."

He sat in bed, resting his back against the elaborate platinum headboard. The Humans were the least of his worries. In fact, he'd gladly trade his problems for their mediocre concerns.

Chapter 5

U nlike King Dubian, Dr. Ezra Barrios found the plight of Humans deeply distressing. He had received orders to complete the last leg of his mission in Austria. However, he was only to observe—never to interfere.

Torn between loyalty to the throne and his conscience, he devised a plan that could change all of their lives forever.

He didn't care what happened to him once he returned to Coldarius. His punishment wouldn't be as bad as not being able to look at his reflection if he stood by and did nothing to stop the Nazis.

Dozens of Human women and children were locked away in a concentration camp waiting to be subjected to horrific experiments. Thousands of dismembered bodies had been cast into shallow graves dug just outside the camp.

Before he left Platirius, he sat with Gallium while packaging hundreds of vials of Callidut—a new substance he'd made to destroy the Kikhanians.

He peered over the rim of his glasses, watching Gallium carefully measure the deep red powder. "I thought you said Callidut wouldn't kill anyone."

Gallium concentrated on shifting the powder into the vials. "I said the version I was working on at the time wouldn't. I've mixed Burkinbach with this formula. It'll kill anything—on any planet. Except for me, of course."

Dr. Barrios observed the vial in his hand before focusing on the endless rows of Callidut resting on a small shelf. "How can you tell which batch is deadly?"

"You can't," said Gallium confidently. "But I can." Giving him a curious glance, he asked, "What's with all the questions, Barrios?"

He licked his dry lips. "Suppose I needed a bit of the Callidut for my mission. Would you be willing to lend me some?"

Gallium observed him for a moment. "Who are you planning to kill?"

He stood looking up at the stars for a moment. "Some Beings don't deserve to live. They commit unspeakable acts—things too despicable to talk about."

Gallium sealed another vial and set it aside. "Is that why you keep having those awful nightmares?"

He nodded. "I hadn't realized you noticed."

Gallium's hand stilled. "I've noticed. Does King Carlomon know what you're planning to do?"

"No, and he doesn't need to. He believes all Humans can be saved if they're shown enough love and compassion, but he's wrong. Some Beings are just evil. No amount of patience or understanding will change them."

Gallium noted his behavior had become increasingly erratic since returning from his previous mission. Sometimes, he screamed out into the night or fought unseen enemies that plagued his dreams. He never spoke of what he did while on Earth, but Gallium suspected he'd seen things he hoped he never would.

"I'll give you whatever you need. Just be discreet about it. Making Callidut—or any drug—comes easily to me." He paused to count what he'd packaged. "You'll only need a small amount. I can easily replace what I give you."

Dr. Barrios turned and placed a hand on his shoulder. "Thank you, Gallium. You don't know how much that means to me!"

Gallium patted his hand. "I suspect you'll put it to good use." He handed a couple of the vials to him. "Always wear gloves when you handle it. Don't inhale it or consume it. I'd lose my mind if anything happened to you."

He looked up at him. "Once you do this, there's no going back, Barrios. Are you prepared for the consequences of taking lives?"

"I'm more than ready," said Dr. Barrios. "I've thought long and hard about what I have to do. If I could take out Hitler, I would, but he always has too many soldiers around. The Human Jews are being slaughtered out of hatred and madness."

Angrily, he kicked at the grass. "They're just...dying for nothing. I'm the furthest thing from perfection, but if I don't do something, I'll never be able to live with myself."

Gallium nodded. "You do what you feel is right. The One will be with you to protect you."

Now Dr. Barrios stood outside the camp, listening to the loud, rough laughter of the German soldiers. They thought he was an Italian doctor sent to treat them. They'd soon find out just how wrong they were.

He wrinkled his nose at the aromas of the evening meal and smiled. He couldn't have planned it more perfectly.

Without making a sound, he snuck into the small kitchen. On high alert, he quickly emptied one of the vials of Callidut into the large soup pot and the other into a jug of wine sitting on a wooden counter.

Then he left before anyone noticed him. Spying a small shed directly across from the camp, he rigged the lock and hid inside to wait.

Soon, their booming, obscene talk echoed out the windows. He hunkered down and folded his hands in his lap. It was winter, but the weather didn't bother him. Earth's winters were mild compared to Coldarius's bitter winds and below freezing temperatures.

A few moments passed before he heard the first screams. He raised his body up to peer over the windowsill of the shed. The soldiers were clutching their throats and falling on top of each other.

Then...it was quiet. He crept to a window and looked inside. All the soldiers lay dead on the floor. It was time. He sprinted across the field to the door of a dilapidated barn and broke the lock. A few of the Human women screamed when they saw him.

He spoke in their language. "I'm not here to hurt you. I'm going to help you. Please listen to me—I'm not like the soldiers. I'll take you where all of you will be safe, but you must come with me now. Please hurry! We don't have much time!"

Tentatively, they looked around at each other. Gradually, they started moving closer to him.

"Yes, that's right," he coaxed. "Come with me." He led them into a large field. "Thank you for trusting me," he told them. "This will be my last mission. I'm so sorry for all the suffering you've gone through. But it's all over now. Very soon you'll all be free. Please close your eyes for a moment."

Once they did as he asked, he forced his mind to concentrate. Like Gallium, he too had a secret no one knew about. He willed his mind to transport them to another destination.

"You can open your eyes," he said.

They opened their eyes and looked around curiously. "Welcome to Argentina. I promised I'd bring you to safety, and I have," he said softly. "It'll be a huge adjustment at first, but in time, you'll carve out new lives for yourselves."

He looked around at all of them, hoping they understood they could never return to Austria. "You'll never have to worry about anyone hurting you again."

His language was rough and broken, but the women understood him perfectly. They hugged, laughed, and cried together. The children yelled and jumped around, elated to be free from the Nazis. Curious onlookers gathered around, but a woman with black hair wound tightly into a knot passed by them and stood next to him.

"Hi, Olivia! These are the friends I told you about," he told her.

He turned back to them. "This is my friend Olivia. She'll help all of you start over. Don't worry about anything—everything will be all right. Here, I have something for all of you."

He went to each woman and gave her a large bag of gold and diamonds. "This is more than enough to start new lives. They took away your Male—I mean, your husbands, but you still have your children. You're free to live however you want now."

They took the bags, bursting into tears again. Deborah Rosenberg touched his arm. "I thought God had forgotten me. I prayed and prayed. Finally, He sent one of His angels."

He grudgingly accepted a few hugs and shook hands with each of the children.

Eden Gershon clung to the edge of his sleeve. "Will we ever see you again?" she asked tearfully.

He lowered his head for a moment, then shook it. "No. But I hope you'll never forget me." He was surprised to find himself choking back tears. He was also surprised he'd grown to care about the Jewish Humans—much more than he ever thought he could. "I'll never forget any of your faces. Promise me you'll live good lives."

"We promise," said Esther Levy. "Thanks to you, we'll live to see our children's children. We'll never forget how you saved us. May God bless you, Dr. Amato."

Time stood still as he carefully scanned their faces, not wanting to miss a detail. "May The One bless you as well." He turned to Olivia again. "Gracias, mi amiga."

"Gracias, Dr. Amato. Don't worry, I'll take good care of them. We've had many friends from Austria and other places come here. You did right to bring them."

He didn't trust himself to speak. He wasn't an overly emotional Being, but witnessing numerous atrocities committed by the Nazis had taken a toll on him. Even if he was punished for disobeying King Carlomon, risking his life to free them was well worth it.

He turned away and got lost in the crowd before transporting himself back to Platirius.

The long years he'd spent in Germany had been draining. The seemingly endless torture and murders were more than he could bear. Gallium hadn't realized he'd been stealing some of the non-lethal version of Callidut to cope with the memories and nightmares—or maybe he had.

Either way, he hadn't confronted him about it, and he was beyond grateful. He needed it. It was the only thing that helped him escape from his mental anguish.

It had been difficult to shoulder the burden alone. He never talked about what he'd witnessed on Earth—not even with King Carlomon. How could he express watching numerous Humans die for unjustifiable reasons?

He hoped he could sleep better knowing he'd finally done something to help. Then, maybe he wouldn't have to rely on Callidut just to make it through the day.

The version he fancied lulled his senses, making him calmer. He was thankful he hadn't experienced hallucinations or excessive hunger. Otherwise, someone other than Queen Dellah would've suspected he'd been taking it.

Learning she discovered his secret terrified him. What if his parents found out? He didn't want to let them, Gallium, or King Carlomon down, but he wasn't strong enough to handle the trauma he'd been exposed to without it.

He wasn't sorry his final mission had ended. As far as he was concerned, if he never saw Earth again, that suited him just fine.

The announcer's animated voice reverberated through the vast dining hall. "Introducing the King and Queen of Platirius, King Dubian and Queen Dellah!"

Greetings filled the air as they descended the stairs of the grand ballroom of King Micah and Queen Marietta of Maieman.

The Queen of Platirius looked stunning in a sheer, strapless gown covered in the tiniest diamonds. A striking high crown covered in sapphires and diamonds sat atop flowing locks. She was the admiration and dream of everyone in attendance—especially the MaleForms.

General Borhaltz slid beside her at the buffet table while King Dubian and King Micah discussed politics at the head of the dining table. "The thought of a beautiful creature like you being on the arm of that hideous King Dubian is enough to make a MaleForm slit his wrist."

Her eyes slid away from the pheasant-stuffed mushroom caps to his scarred and pitted face. "Then you should get on with it, since I'll never be on yours."

His booming laugh filled the chamber. "So the reports are true. You're the steel behind Platirius's military, not your husband."

She placed a lamb chop next to the mushrooms. "I've never known you to be one who'd listen to idle gossip, General. I assure you, my husband is quite capable of leading Platirius without my assistance."

His greedy eyes devoured the alluring curves of her bosom. "Oh, I doubt that. He's sitting on the throne, but it doesn't mean he deserves to. Everyone knows how he stabbed Prince Dimaro in the back. Were he alive, you'd be here with him instead of his brother."

"Had he lived, I wouldn't have been here at all. I doubt I would've been able to stomach him long enough to share the same space with him. King Anemi should've stuck to politics, not matchmaking."

He forked up a piece of venison, covering it with thick gravy. "Speaking of King Anemi, he's not around anymore either. Looks like your husband killed two birds with one stone. King Hitam won't be so easy to overthrow."

She added shards of thinly sliced beef to her plate. "Unless you have proof of that, I'd suggest you take your conspiracy theories elsewhere. As for the Kikhanians, who would know about them better than you? You've lost to King Hitam, what? Twice?"

She clucked her tongue. "It must've been difficult to sell your daughter to him so he wouldn't absorb your planet. And what did he do? Sold her to another king so he could marry Queen Amori. She ended up being an unwilling concubine to a stranger. You have no room to try and air out what you think you know of my husband's family drama."

He licked his thin lips. "You're much too pretty to have such a harsh tongue."

She gave him a dazzling smile. "You needn't worry about my tongue. Or anything else on my body." She nodded at the table. "Your poor wife is staring at us like a hawk. You should run along." She whirled around with her loaded plate and sat down next to King Dubian.

"Queen Dellah," said Queen Marietta. "We're so pleased you and King Dubian have joined us tonight. We're very proud of our recruits—especially our son. He graduated from military training a year ago and is undefeated on four planets. Oh! Here he is now."

She waved a tall young MaleForm over to the table. "King Micah and I would like you to meet our son. Say hello, Dear."

He was so tall, Queen Dellah had to crane her neck to look up at him. He bowed and kissed her hand. "Good evening, Queen Dellah and King Dubian. I'm Major Lucian Kron."

A knock at the door awakened Legend. They never had visitors at that hour. Careful not to make a sound, she grabbed her Azgoate and crept down the stairs. Silently, she peeked through the eyehole.

A MaleForm shrouded in a dark hood stood outside. She snatched open the door and pointed the Azgoate into the icy darkness. "State your business or I'll blow your head off!"

He raised his hands in the air. "Is this what I get for fighting my way here from Platirius? A DeathCeremony?"

Her heart racing, she lowered the weapon. He stepped into the foyer and removed the hood.

"Gallium!" she cried, throwing herself into his arms. "I can't believe you're here!"

He laughed and lifted her off the floor. "And I can't believe you'd wave an Azgoate in my face. Now what have I done to deserve that, huh?"

The Azgoate was a model specifically designed to target an enemy's brain. One shot from the nozzle was powerful enough to separate the brain from the skull. That's exactly what she'd planned to do to an unknown intruder.

He set her down on the floor. She reached up and kissed him deeply and received a firm pat on her buttocks. "What's gotten into you, WomanForm? You know we don't have crime on Coldarius."

She sheepishly ducked her head and set the weapon aside. "Well, there's plenty everywhere else. Mother and I live alone. WomenForms can't afford to be too careful these days."

He shook his head slowly. "You're a born warrior, Legend. I wonder what you'd be like as something more docile—like a baker or a painter."

Her golden eyes sparkled under the low lights. "Bakers have rolling pins and painters have sharp points on their brushes. Even the smallest things can be turned into proper weapons."

He threw back his head and laughed. "Never mind. I'll never win against you, will I?"

Her smile calmed his racing thoughts. Life on Platirius was so busy, he rarely had time to relax. He missed the quiet tranquility of Coldarius. He also missed the WomanForm standing before him—much more than he ever dreamed he would.

"Have you heard anything about being accepted into Platirius's army?"

She gave him a gentle push. "Oh? Now you want me to join? Didn't you warn me of the dangers of the detestable Platirian MaleForms who'd prey on poor little old me?"

"I've had a change of heart. As cowardly as some of them are, trust me, I'm not worried about you. You could mop them up like water. It's a good thing more of our soldiers are coming over."

Taking his hand in hers, she led him to the oversized divan. Once he was seated, she laid her head on his chest, inhaling his masculine, woodsy scent. "King Carlomon told us Platirius has lost a lot of soldiers in the war."

He shrugged out of his outerwear and pulled her close to his chest. "Yes, that's true. Queen Dellah is on Maieman with King Dubian to recruit more soldiers into their army." He kissed her forehead. Instinctively, she snuggled closer to him. She couldn't remember a time when she'd felt so safe.

"I spoke with Queen Dellah a couple weeks ago. She said she'd review my application after her InfantForm was born. She's about ready to give birth, so I should be on Platirius by the first season."

She leaned back to look up at him. "That should be a pretty time with all your flowers beginning to bloom. How long can you stay?"

He kissed her, gently nibbling on her bottom lip. "The queen and king won't be back until after a five-day span. I plan to visit with you before getting a room at the inn down the road. I'm leaving on the fourth day."

"An inn? What's wrong with staying here? We have extra rooms, you know?"

"Um, Miss Guilde. I don't think your MotherForm would approve of me staying here."

She frowned at him. "And why not? I'm a grown WomanForm, aren't I? We're not ChildForms anymore!"

"We're not married. I don't want to give Lady Alarah or her busted old friends any leverage to damage your reputation."

She ran her fingers through his hair. "The town whore? Damaging *my* reputation?" She chuckled. "Oh, Gallium, that's just precious."

"I mean it," he said. "Everyone knows how terrible she is, but like minds stick together. She's made more than enough friends on Platirius who can make life very difficult for you. Queen Dellah has your back, but I want to protect you too."

She looked away. "I'm not helpless. I haven't needed looking after since my father died. He's been gone for so many years, I've grown accustomed to being the protector of our family."

He slid the pad of his thumb across her bottom lip. "Well, now you have me! I can only imagine how hard it was for you to grow up without a father. You got used to it and decided that MaleForms aren't needed, but we are."

She smiled when he softly pinched her nose. "Our job is to provide and protect. Those who don't are weak-minded and useless—like King Dubian."

He pulled her closer. She felt amazing in his arms. He wished they could remain that way forever. "They don't deserve recognition. It's why The One created the SexForms. Beings outside of Earth understand this and submit to His will."

He looked up at the stars, grateful for the opportunity to finally spend time with her alone. "It's why we're more advanced than Humans will ever be. Never adopt their rhetoric, Legend. Their world is broken and chaotic with good reason."

She dropped her head. "You're right," she said. "I apologize. I didn't mean to make you feel unneeded."

"Thank you. That means a lot to me. How about I stay for a while, and then I'll go? I'll wait until you get off work tomorrow, and then we'll spend our evening together."

An amused voice chimed in. "That won't be necessary."

Gallium removed his hand from her thigh and jumped up from the duvet. "Mrs. Guilde! Legend and I were just..."

Mrs. Guilde was sitting at the top of the staircase. "Yes, I saw what you and my daughter were doing—talking."

Legend's eyes were a carbon copy of her mother's. "I'm not so old I don't remember how it feels to be in love, young MaleForm. Legend, I can handle the shop on my own. Have fun entertaining your intended. Do you still call each other that these days?"

"But, Mother—"

Mrs. Guilde raised her hand. "Not another word, Legend. He came all the way from Platirius to see you. Cora Gee's inn is very nice, but he shouldn't have to find ways to occupy his time until you're free."

The older WomanForm winked at Gallium. "Keep her out as long as you like, Gallium. And thank you for thinking of her reputation. Amos and Etienne have raised you to be a fine young MaleForm."

Legend bit her lip while Gallium blushed.

Mrs. Guilde smiled at them. "Well, I think I'll turn in now. In a while."

"In a while," said Gallium and Legend.

"Well, I guess that settles that. What shall we do tomorrow?"

"Anything you want," he told her.

Her eyes sparkled.

"Anything but that!"

She pouted. "You're so prudish, Gallium."

The heat simmering in his gaze made her breath catch. "When you're my wife, prudish is the last thing you'll think when you see me," he promised.

She raised an eyebrow. "What kind of proposal is that?"

"It's coming," he said. "I think we both know there's no one I want except you. Give me time to get a proper ring for you and I'll make it happen."

She sang, "I've seen the glory of Coldarius-Platirius. I've even seen the splendor of Platz. But nothing will ever make me happier...than when Gallium puts me on my back!"

"Legend!" Gallium whispered fiercely. He swung a panicked glance in the direction of the staircase.

She laughed. "Mother is resting. Even if she isn't, she knows exactly how my mind works."

"What a naughty WomanForm you are, Legend Guilde!"

She crossed her supple thigh. "When I'm your wife, you'll find out exactly how naughty I am!"

He didn't doubt it. Not for a minute.

"Y ou're so young to be a soldier. Just fifteen summers," said Queen Dellah. "How have you managed to maintain such an impressive record, Major Kron? Who was your mentor?"

He grinned at her. "I don't have a mentor. I just listened well to our instructors and developed my own fighting techniques to conquer our enemies. I've also trained three junior soldiers to follow in my footsteps once I relocate out of Maieman."

He nodded in the direction of three officers seated at another table. "I don't want to worry about my ParentForms being in danger without me being here. I don't intend for any army I lead to be defeated."

Queen Dellah and King Dubian shared a glance. King Micah looked from them to Major Kron. "Our son is a prodigy. He has a natural gift for battle. You won't find a finer warrior in all the galaxy."

Placing a hand on Major Kron's shoulder, he said, "I'm not just saying that because he's my son. It's the truth."

"But why have him leave?" asked King Dubian. "If he were my son, I wouldn't allow him to."

"We don't place limitations on our sons," said King Micah. "They're free to go where they please—except Earth. The Humans don't deserve our superior abilities. Let them rot."

Queen Dellah raised her glass in agreement and everyone at the table followed suit, toasting King Micah's declaration.

"And as Lucian said, he'll be leaving us in very capable hands," said King Micah. "Were he to stay, he couldn't go up the ranks without someone accusing us of giving him titles instead of earning them. We want his career to go as far as it may go. Our second son will take my place as king after I pass on."

King Dubian's grip tightened on his dining utensil. Quickly, he cut into his steak before anyone noticed.

Queen Dellah noticed but pretended she didn't. "Major Kron, we'd love for you to join us on Platirius. My husband and I have selected ten thousand of your father's troops. It would be a shame if you weren't among them."

He nodded eagerly. "I'd love to. I'm very interested in the war going on between Platirius and Kikhani. If General Sodom wouldn't mind, maybe I could give him some pointers?"

"He'll take any advice he's given," said King Dubian dryly. "Thank you, Major Kron. My wife and I are happy to have you aboard."

Major Kron raised his glass again. "Thank you for having confidence in my abilities. I'm looking forward to joining Platirius."

"Here's to a long and prosperous future between Platirius and Maieman," said Queen Dellah.

"Hear, hear! I wish for long life and prosperity for all of us!" said King Micah.

Gallium helped Dr. Barrios pack medical supplies and Callidut to send to the Platirian soldiers based on Kikhani. "How did things go with you and that pretty soldier?" asked Dr. Barrios.

Gallium sealed up a box. "Her name is Legend. And they went very well, thank you."

Dr. Barrios shot him a sly look. "Oh? How well?"

He threw a roll of bandages at him. "Mind your business, Barrios. She's not that kind of WomanForm."

"With a figure like that, I'm not surprised her name is Legend. Don't tell me she's a prude!"

Gallium thought of his time spent with her on Coldarius and smiled. "I'm not telling you anything. Get your own WomanForm."

Dr. Barrios sighed. "When would I find the time? Gallium, did you know oranges are round on Earth?"

He looked up at him. "What? I can't even imagine that."

Dr. Barrios nodded. "It's true! Their food looks so strange and it tastes even stranger. Here our potatoes are shaped like their triangles. They'd call our tomatoes and oranges squares and our ears of corn, crescents."

He packed another carton of bandages into a box. "And much of their food is deep fried in something called lard or vegetable oil. Lard is made from pork fat, but they seep oil from soybeans."

"Then why call it vegetable oil instead of soybean oil?"

"I have no idea, but it and lard can kill them off."

"How?"

"Well, it's high in saturated fat. That raises bad cholesterol, which puts them at risk of coronary artery disease and makes their weight fluctuate. Neither has any effect on us. I've eaten tons of deep-fried meat and other things and haven't gained anything. "

Gallium rolled up a bandage and tossed it inside a crate. "If they're aware the oil or fat or whatever you call it is bad for them, why do they use it?"

"Some don't, but many of them do. We don't have the health problems they have."

"We don't have anything the Humans have," said Gallium sagely.

"That's true. Lard is thick, white, and feels... I can't compare it to anything we have. I ate a spoonful of it and gagged."
He chuckled. "Want to hear something funny? Our chicken is cylinder and boneless, but Humans cut chicken into odd-shaped parts. They eat it right off the bone."

Gallium stared at him. "They eat meat with bones still in it like animals? I can't imagine that!"

"It's not bad, but it's not better than ours. Their doughnuts are round with holes in the middle, but ours are shaped like their letter 'g.'"

"Upper or lowercase?" asked Gallium.

Dr. Barrios smirked. "Lowercase."

Gallium looked up at the stars and sighed. "Humans are strange."

Dr. Barrios cackled. "Yes, they are! Let's get these crates loaded on the crafts."

"We don't need to. All we had to do was pack the supplies. Queen Dellah ordered the other soldiers to load them."

Dr. Barrios wiped his brow and sat down on the ground. "Many thanks to her! How about we go and have some delicious cylinder chicken?"

Gallium stood and extended his hand. Pulling him to his feet, he said, "That's the best advice I've heard all day."

Chapter 6

Dr. Krause, Queen Dellah's personal physician, placed her on bed rest until the new InfantForm's birth. King Dubian was frantic. He ordered her to be at his disposal day and night to answer his never-ending questions.

"What's wrong with her? Will she and the InfantForm be all right?"

Dr. Krause checked her pulse. "This is just a precautionary measure, Your Highness. We want Her Majesty to give birth in the safest manner possible."

He glared at the young doctor. "That's not what I asked," he snapped.

Queen Dellah rolled her eyes toward the Heavens. "Dubian, you posed a question and she answered it. Berating her won't change anything. I don't like it, but if it's what she suggests, I'm willing to do what's necessary."

She looked from him to Dr. Krause. "Just how long do I have to stay off my feet, Dr. Krause?"

She cleared her throat nervously. "At least for another month, My Queen. May I listen to your heartbeat?"

King Dubian assisted her to sit up on the bed. "I thought it wouldn't take longer than a couple weeks! I can't be out of commission that long. We're at war!"

She listened to her heart rate and recorded it before she responded. "I understand, Your Highness. However, my top priority is to ensure you have a safe delivery. I can't do it without your assistance."

"I'll assume responsibility of the military," said King Dubian. "Having Major Kron aboard has allowed us to cut King Hitam's army in half."

She mulled that over. "I want Gallium to be over Major Kron. General Iham will assist him."

He gaped at her. "Gallium? He's not a soldier. What on Platirius can he do?"

She narrowed her eyes at him. "Much more than you can, my dear husband. I don't believe I asked a question, Dubian, I gave my order. I've already told you he has unique abilities. We need him to fight."

She shifted around until she found a comfortable spot on the bed. "Besides, he's older than Major Kron. He may be a talented soldier, but I'm not willing to let Platirius's fate rest in the hands of a Being who is only fifteen summers."

He clapped his hands together. "Then let's send Gallium to Kikhani. I'll make the preparations right now."

Dr. Krause stifled a laugh when she grabbed his collar and pulled him down on the bed. "You'll do no such thing, you fool. There's no reason to dispatch Gallium to Kikhani. Besides,

General Sodom and most of our troops are there. If we send him, we're wide open for a sneak attack here—not just from the Kikhanians, but from other realms too."

She stared pityingly at him. "You have no idea how to command an army, but I do. Mark my words. We need him to stay on Platirius."

Breathing harshly, Major Kron rushed into the medical chamber. "Queen Dellah, the Kikhanians are bearing down on us! Do you want me to head up the counterattack?"

"Calm down," snapped King Dubian. "You report to me now. My wife will assume leadership once the new InfantForm arrives."

Major Kron looked from him to Queen Dellah. "It's all right, Major Kron. What the king says is true. However, I want you to counterstrike—on Gallium's command. If he needs you, he'll let you know." She pressed a button next to the bed. "Gallium? Are you there?"

"I'm here, Your Highness. We have Kikhanians on the radar about twelve yards out. I smelled them coming before they entered our territory."

"Good. Let them land, then finish them off. Major Kron and the rest of the soldiers will dispose of the bodies."

"Roger that, Queen Dellah."

King Dubian looked from her to Major Kron. "What does he mean he smelled them?"

She positioned a pillow behind her back and turned on her side. "One of Gallium's abilities is smelling the oxygen in plants and in us. He can control it too."

She ignored their stunned reactions. "Get out there and observe him. Major Kron, General Iham will hold the troops back until he's finished." She looked him in the eye. "Don't get in their way. Have I been heard?"

Major Kron bowed to her. "Yes, Your Highness!"

"Dubian, I expect a full report when it's over," she said, adjusting the covers around her large belly.

"Of course, My Queen. Don't worry. Let's go, Major Kron."

Maybe I don't need to worry about Gallium. Perhaps the Kikhanians are the answer to my prayers. Then the tension between her and I will cease.

King Dubian hoped so. For the sake of his marriage, he certainly hoped the Kikhanians would kill Gallium.

General Iham had served in Coldarius's army since the death of King Carlomon's father. Platirius had lost many soldiers on Kikhani, but Queen Dellah allowed the Coldarian troops to stay behind.

Secretly, she had hoped to weed out most of the Platirians so that the army would be comprised primarily of Coldarians. Her plan succeeded. With Gallium in charge, victory was inevitable for Platirius. That is, as long as her idiotic husband didn't interfere.

General Iham stood with Gallium, watching the Kikhanians slowly walk across the field. "Gallium, they've all landed and are advancing now."

He raised his arm to signal for the troops to raise their weapons.

"That won't be needed, General," said Gallium quietly.

He stared at him. "You'll need reinforcements. You can't fight them bare-handed, son."

Gallium kept his eyes trained on the Kikhanian soldiers. "I have my weapons. On my signal, order everyone to put on their masks."

Perplexed, General Iham nodded. He looked around at the dozens of acres of JunipBuds they were standing in. Gallium waited until the Kikhanians were nearly halfway across the field.

"It's time."

Once General Iham put on his mask and signaled for the troops to put on theirs, Gallium inhaled a deep breath and raised his arms. Fascinated, General Iham watched as he used his nose and mouth to extract the almost translucent venom of the JunipBuds from the plants.

The older general stepped back in terror when Gallium inhaled the venom. Ingesting the deadly liquid inside the JunipBuds was a sure way to die, but he opened his eyes, held out his hands, and expelled the poison across the field and into the Kikhanians.

They screamed when it entered their bloodstreams, producing clusters of painful boils and blisters on their skin. He continued blowing in the direction of the soldiers until the last of the venom left his lungs. Five thousand troops fell to the ground. King Dubian nearly fainted.

Everyone stood fixated on Gallium. An eerie silence hung over the field. He turned to look at the cowardly king. "Our enemies have been eradicated, Your Highness. How would you like for us to proceed?"

Struggling to catch his breath, he wanted to escape the hate burning in Gallium's eyes but couldn't. Although he knew it was impossible, he thought he read the younger Coldarian's mind. *I could kill you anytime I want to.* His terrifying nightmare came flooding back.

They were waiting for his next command, but he couldn't make his mouth move. He'd witnessed with his own eyes what Gallium was capable of, but he still couldn't believe it.

Gallium looked up at a high window. Queen Dellah, bolstered up by Dr. Krause, was watching from above. She'd seen everything. Her proud smile warmed his heart. She peered over the edge of the windowsill, staring down at King Dubian.

Her red, manicured nails tapped impatiently on the windowsill. "Are you going to give him an answer? We have bodies to clear off our lands."

Startled, he looked up to where she stood before training his eyes on Gallium again.

"Major Kron," he said shakily.

Major Kron, still staring at Gallium, hadn't realized he'd been holding his breath. "Yes, King Dubian?" he whispered.

"Assist General Iham to get the bodies into the crafts and send them back to King Hitam."

He saluted him. "Yes, King Dubian!"

"Major Kron can mobilize the troops and handle disposing of the bodies on his own," said Queen Dellah. "General Iham? I'd like to see you and Gallium in my bed chamber now, please?"

The soldiers backed away from Gallium as he approached the palace.

"What's this?" she snapped. "He's a Coldarian. One of our own! He just saved all of your hides, but you're acting as if he's contagious! Is that how you show proper respect to General Barrios?" Immediately, the soldiers began saluting him. "That's better! If I ever see such disrespect shown to him again, you'll be shipped out of here like the Kikhanians."

Her eyes looked as if they were cut from brilliant diamonds. Major Kron stilled as her icy gaze swept over him. "Major Kron. The Kikhanians's odor is repulsive enough to make me vomit. Tend to your duties, please."

His salute was crisp and quick. While he and the soldiers hurried to remove the bodies, King Dubian, General Iham, and Gallium walked side by side through the palace doors. No one said a word until they were in front of her.

"You know I respect you, General Iham. Forgive me for not telling you sooner, but I couldn't reveal Gallium's capabilities until the time was right."

She looked over at the soldiers dragging the dead Kikhanians into the crafts. "I couldn't have asked for a more perfect time than this. Now, only a fourth of King Hitam's army remains. I've arranged it so no other planets would send more troops to his aid. If we can absorb Kikhani into Platirius, the power we'd inherit would be astronomical."

General Iham cleared his throat. "I have always trusted your judgment. I admit his—power gave me a fright, but I'm glad he's on our side."

She looked over at Gallium and beamed at him. "So am I," she said happily. "Send word to all of our media outlets. I want the entire galaxy to know Platirius's military is undefeatable. If any Being so much as lies down and dreams of beating my army, they'd better wake up and bow to me."

She flexed her little toes under the covers. "I want pictures taken of the bodies before they're shipped off and posted on all the major media outlets. Let all the realms know who's on top. Today. Tomorrow. Forever."

General Iham bowed to her. "We'll get it done, Your Highness. You can count on us."

"I know, and I thank you. That was an impressive scene out there, General Barrios. Is there anything you'd like to add before I dismiss you? Are you well?"

"Thank you, Your Majesty. I feel fine."

She winked at him. "Good. How about you, Dubian?"

He slid his eyes off Gallium toward her. "What will we do about the rest of King Hitam's army?"

"I've sent lethal doses of Callidut to our troops on Kikhani," she said. "They'll use it to wipe out the rest of his troops. I had hoped King Hitam would send some of them here so I could have an estimate of how many he had left."

She grabbed a pillow and handed it to her husband. He hastened to place it under her feet. She adjusted them on the pillow and lay back against the headboard.

"Looks like he granted my wish. He spared five thousand for this mission. His plan was to attack us by surprise, eliminate the reinforcements, and finish off what was left of us on Kikhani."

She chuckled. "Once again, he underestimated us. After we annihilate his troops, he'll have no choice but to surrender. Now, thanks to General Barrios, we've had a fine source of entertainment for the day. I'm looking forward to watching a replay of today's events on the TranScreen tonight. Dubian, please let the surveillance team know I want all of my calls held until tomorrow."

She yawned and nodded to her husband. "I can't wait to share the good news with my father. It's time for me to take a nap. In a while, MaleForms."

"In a while, Queen Dellah," they said.

The next day, Queen Dellah was enjoying a long-awaited walk around the palace gardens. She held on to King Dubian's elbow to help with her balance.

"Dr. Krause said you should rest, Dear," he said. "I don't think it's appropriate for you to be up and about."

She looked at him out of the corner of her eye. "I'm taking a walk, not sprinting across the galaxy for a prize."

Little Dancie Ambers ran up to them. "Hello, Queen Dellah! I picked a pretty flower for you."

"She doesn't need that!" snapped King Dubian. "She has acres of flowers. Go away and leave her alone!"

When Dancie's face crumpled, he barked, "And don't start blubbering! I don't want to hear it."

He wilted under his wife's chilly stare. "Did the ChildForm address you or I, My King? As for blubbering, if I were you, I'd close my mouth. If you don't have anything nice to say to our subjects, then say nothing."

She bent down to Dancie. "What is it you have for me, little one? Oh, what a pretty rose! These are my favorite, you know? You're so smart, Dancie Ambers!"

The little ChildForm's confidence was instantly restored. She beamed up at the beautiful queen.

"Would you like to put it in my hair?"

Dancie nodded shyly and reached up to place the flower in her hair.

"Dancie! What are you doing?"

Her mother, Avi Ambers, ran up to her. "You know you're not allowed to touch Queen Dellah!" she scolded.

She frowned at her. "I don't recall saying that, Avi Ambers. Do you? Where did you get the notion I'm too valuable to be touched?"

Avi's eyes darted to King Dubian, then quickly away before bowing. "Forgive me, Queen Dellah."

"The ChildForm just made me look beautiful today. You should be proud to be rearing such a sweet little Being. How's your FatherForm?"

Avi's head snapped up. "Oh? Thank you, Your Highness! He's in good health, thank you for asking."

She nodded. "Of course. Please tell him I'd like a few dozen of his best tomatoes to be brought to the dining chamber just for me when he has time. I know how busy the harvest season gets. Dr. Krause says I need to eat more salads."

"Oh, he'll make time for you, My Queen." She took Darcie's hand. "I'll go and tell him right now!"

Queen Dellah stroked Dancie's hair. "I appreciate that, Avi. Bye, bye, little one. Please return to see me once my baby is born, yes? Avi, please stop by the royal dining chamber and tell Dora Reese I said to give Dancie a dozen of those hazelnut toffee cookies she baked this morning."

Her warm eyes looked down at Dancie again. "She can share them with her friends at school tomorrow."

Tears of gratitude shone in Avi's eyes. "Thank you, Your Highness. We wish you and your new baby many blessings!" She paused uncomfortably and bowed to King Dubian. "May The One bless your beautiful family, King Dubian."

He smiled stiffly yet said nothing. Avi hurried away with her daughter while he avoided Queen Dellah's disgusted gaze.

"Would it kill you to show respect to others? Just once?"

"Please be patient with me. It's difficult for me to open up to the common—to others."

She shook her head. "You've been singing that same tired old song for years. You may be the King of Platirius, but that doesn't give you the right to look down your nose at anyone. Berating a ChildForm for giving me a flower? Scaring her MotherForm out of her mind? That's not the legacy I want to be remembered for. If you want to bear that cross, you'll do it alone."

She straightened the flower in her hair and left him standing. Ducking his head, he quickened his long strides to catch up with her short, brisk ones.

She nodded to a neatly dressed WomanForm. A large, yellow hat rested on her head. "Hello, Marcia Blight! How are things going in the fashion chamber?"

Marcia smiled and bowed to her. "As busy as ever, My Queen. When you can spare a moment, I have bolts of fabric I'd like you to look at. We've sent over thirty day gowns for you to wear once the new InfantForm is born."

"That's very generous of you, Marcia. Thank you for thinking of me."

"We always keep you in mind when we create new pieces," said Marcia. "You're the most fashionable royal figure Platirius has ever had." Giving King Dubian a side glance, she said, "Queen Zherta had the most dreadful taste in clothes."

She extended her hand to Marcia. "So I've heard. That's grand praise. I hope I can live up to everyone's expectations."

Marcia accepted her hand, shook it carefully, then bowed. "We wish you a long life, Queen Dellah."

King Dubian noted she had said nothing to him. Inwardly, he fumed. Without his wife's knowledge, he had sent Marcia's husband, Wilkus Blight, to the mines to retrieve a large diamond for her. She had ordered the mine to be closed until it could be safely updated.

It was one of the few tasks she'd allowed him to handle. Since concern for the welfare of the Platirians wasn't a priority, he never followed through. Once Wilkus had extracted it from the wall, he unknowingly weakened the structure.

He was at the entrance when the roof collapsed on top of him—one hand sticking out, still clutching the diamond. King Dubian had dispatched a soldier to retrieve the diamond, but left Wilkus to suffocate to death. He ordered everyone not to tell his wife what happened.

Marcia was heartbroken that her husband's body had been left to decompose. Summoning courage, she tearfully pleaded with the queen to allow her to have it removed. Queen Dellah had no idea what happened to Wilkus.

She railed at him in front of everyone and held a proper burial service for Wilkus in the royal worship chamber. It was the first time a commoner had received such an honor. To his horror, she refused to accept the diamond and had it buried with Wilkus. Under her watch, the mine was repaired immediately.

Marcia had never forgiven him nor had any of his subjects. Everyone despised him and he knew it. It was his own doing, but his cavalier personality made accepting their contempt difficult. Marcia bowed again, keeping her eyes on the ground.

"A long life to you as well, King Dubian."

Her contumelious behavior offended him, but not wanting to annoy the queen any further, he nodded curtly and walked away. During the rest of her walk, she greeted every subject as if they were family.

She asked about their families, school, and whether they were satisfied with their jobs. She was pleased when they reported they didn't lack food or proper medical care.

Finally, the success she and her father had achieved on Coldarius had been brought to the Platirians. She had intimate knowledge about everyone and made them feel as if they mattered.

Her kindness had never gone unnoticed, nor was it taken for granted. While her subjects wished death on her husband, they genuinely loved and appreciated her.

She accepted every flower the ChildForms gave her, rewarding them with smiles, pats on the head, and delicious treats. By the time they reached the palace, she had a large bouquet.

"Ashna," she called to a cleaning staff. "Place these in one of my best vases and have it brought up to my bed chamber. I'd like them to sit by the nearest window so the sun shines on them each morning."

"Yes, My Queen. I'll bring them up shortly."

"Thank you, Ashna." She turned to him. "I think I'll take a walk every morning. It's better than lying around all day and makes me feel more energized. Speaking with our Beings makes me happy too."

"Whatever you think is best, Dellah. I'll support it."

"Speaking of support, the mine is holding up nicely, don't you think?"

He winced at the acerbic dig, but was more moved by her disapproval of him than Wilkus's death. For him, Wilkus was a paltry bug that got crushed—he saw no reason to reflect on what he'd done.

"Now that the walls are restructured, I'd like a new bracelet to be designed for Queen Pia. I'd like to congratulate her on the birth of her new InfantForm."

He helped her to the bed and arranged the covers around her. "It'll be done right away, My Queen."

It was difficult to tell what she was thinking, for Platirians couldn't read the minds of Coldarians. "I hope it'll be done faster than you repaired the mine. We must keep our alliances with other planets open to continue trading."

He bowed to her. "I'll go and personally see to it."

"Thank you," she said stiffly.

The cold demeanor he'd shown their subjects had deeply upset her. She realized the kind behavior he'd demonstrated in the first years of their marriage had been an act. While they were dating, she hadn't thought it was possible, but she'd come to regret marrying him.

The merger had been beyond prosperous for Coldarius, but at what cost? Still, the Platirians were better off with her as their leader. They rested comfortably in their beds at night knowing she was a buffer between them and her husband's penchant for apathy.

She didn't want to imagine how things would change if she were no longer around. She snuggled into the covers, trying to ignore the pain throbbing in her womb. Things would be all right once the baby arrived. Surely The One wouldn't take her away from her ChildForms and everyone who needed her.

There was no question Platirius would fall without her. She hugged her pillow tightly to her chest, praying He would spare her life.

"We never thought you had that kind of power, General Barrios," said Sergeant Lionus.

"Oh, cut the 'general' bull," snapped Gallium. "The queen isn't around. You don't need to call me that!"

He was very uncomfortable with the new title and all the attention he'd gained since killing the Kikhanians.

Sergeant Lionus shook his head. "Sorry, but what she says goes. And she just appointed you as general. Addressing you formally is how we show respect."

"Then show it by doing what I ask. I'm one of you—no better, no worse."

Corporal Canob said, "You could be the king if you wanted, Gallium—I mean, General Barrios! You could kill King Dubian just like you did the Kikhanians!" He cocked his head. "Why haven't you?"

"I don't want to be king. I'm neither royalty nor a soldier. I'm a gardener. I've never wanted to do anything besides what I'm doing."

Sergeant Lionus sighed. "It would be better taking orders from you than that fool! He had us surrounding the border, waiting for more Kikhanians to arrive. You killed off most of his army and the rest are on Kikhani. Who would be crazy enough to send more soldiers just to die? He doesn't know what he's doing!"

"I know that, and you know that, but what can we do? Until Queen Dellah is back, we have to follow his commands."

"What are you all doing standing about?" asked Major Kron.

Incensed by his imperious tone, the soldiers glared at him but kept silent. Unlike them, he showed genuine respect to King Dubian. On top of that, he'd been given a high position they felt he hadn't earned.

He was a wealthy, spoon-fed MaleForm from Maieman—not Coldarius or Platirius. Still, he was permitted to boss around soldiers who'd worked longer and harder since before he was born. They hated him almost as much as they hated the king.

Sensing their antipathy, he carefully chose his next words. Any one of them—especially Gallium—could easily kill him and the others would look the other way. He had plans for his future—he couldn't afford to allow their petty grievances against the king to jeopardize them.

"I'd like to thank all of you for your hard work today. I didn't expect to get them all cleared away and shipped off, but you completed the task without complaining."

He cleared his throat as the uncomfortable silence grew heavy. Out of the corner of his eye, he spied a few Platirian soldiers.

"I hear we'll have WomenForm soldiers joining us soon. That should be interesting." He was well aware that some of the Platirian MaleForms despised WomenForms, but not the Coldarians, so he kept his tone neutral.

One of the Platirian soldiers spat on the ground. "We have enough to do without babysitting them. They should be cooking and cleaning, not running around with weapons. Who's to say they won't accidentally blow one of our heads off?"

"You sound ignorant and dumb," said Gallium coldly. "The queen was our general for many years and our record is still undefeated. With her at Platirius's helm, only King Hitam has been crazy enough to challenge us. That's because he doesn't respect WomenForms either. You think Platirius would be invincible if King Dubian didn't have her by his side?"

The soldiers looked around at each other, but Gallium looked steadily at Major Kron. He hadn't fooled him. He knew he was trying to use WomenForms as a scapegoat to divert their hatred away from him.

Silently, they assessed each other. Major Kron held his breath. He didn't mind being hated by the other soldiers—he could deal with that. But Gallium was different. Although he feared and despised him, he was careful not to let it show.

"I'm sure you have some things to do for King Dubian, Major," said Gallium. "Don't let us keep you."

He got the hint. They didn't want him around. He offered Gallium a quick salute. "Good night, General Barrios."

Corporal Canob looked at his retreating back and spit on the ground. "You think he heard us?"

"Even if he did, if he runs to tattle to the king, there's nothing either of them can do about it," said Gallium.

Sergeant Lionus watched Major Kron in disgust. "He's barely old enough to shave, but we have to take orders from him."

"He's under General Iham, so in my book, he's an afterthought. Just let him think he's running things," said Gallium, standing up and stretching. "I'm going to turn in. I agree with him about one thing—you did an outstanding job today. Let's keep it going until we defeat Kikhani."

Loud cheers rang from the military chamber. Major Kron turned to look back at the soldiers. They wanted nothing to do with him. Well, he was fine with that. One day, it would be his turn to show them what he could do. When he did, no one would look down on him ever again.

Chapter 7

Gallium shifted the bundle of packages in his arms to scan his hand across the TeleShield. He and his family were anticipating celebrating JehovRi, the annual LifeCelebration of The One.

It was his favorite festive event of the year. JehovRi lasted for five days. The Coldarians exchanged gifts, made homemade wine, and prepared a huge feast to be shared with family and friends.

It was suspected Queen Dellah wouldn't be able to make the journey this year. While the Coldarians would miss her presence, they were relieved they wouldn't have to spend their celebration with King Dubian.

"Barrios, could you give me a hand here?" asked Gallium.

Dr. Barrios retrieved a mound of gifts from him and ushered into the open doorway. Etienne came running to assist them.

"Ezra! Gallium! By The One, we thought you wouldn't be able to make it this year! I'm so happy to see you both." She peered around them. "Is Queen Dellah coming?"

They shared a look. Queen Dellah hadn't wanted many to know she was on bed rest. "We don't know," said Dr. Barrios.

"She's been very busy with the war going on. I'm sure if she doesn't make it, it's for good reason."

Amos appeared from the cottage's spacious dining chamber. He observed Gallium for a long time, struggling to find the right words. Gallium braced himself and waited for his father to say something. Although he looked forward to spending time with his family, he wasn't ready to deal with the litany of questions about his abilities.

Etienne sensed the tension in the room and looked from her son to her husband. Gently, she pinched his arm. "Now isn't the time," she mouthed.

Amos cleared his throat and nodded. "I don't expect the weather to be as bitter as it was last year. Maybe we'll be able to roast the pheasants on spits instead of cooking them inside."

Dr. Barrios poured himself and Gallium steaming cups of tea made with apples, cinnamon, and ginger. "Ah, that would be nice! I've always loved the smell of meat cooking in the open air."

Gallium took the cup from him, quietly sipping the excellently brewed tea.

Etienne placed a large platter of cookies and small pastries beside the pitcher of tea. "Legend and Mrs. Guilde will be over shortly. Mrs. Guilde made her signature cheese pies. I can't wait to eat a slice!"

Thoughts of Legend comforted Gallium. It would be nice to sit with her by the roaring fire, not worrying about war or King Dubian's antics. He prayed she wouldn't be put off by his powers. He couldn't imagine his life without her.

The scanner buzzed again. This time it was Legend bustling through the door with Mrs. Guilde. He held his breath when their eyes met. It was now or never.

"Well, if it isn't our hero coming home to bless us with his presence. I heard you took out the Kikhanians with a single breath! I wish I could've seen it!"

Anxiety seized him, causing his hand to shake. Quickly, he set down the tea to avoid burning himself.

Mrs. Guilde said, "Legend."

Legend looked at her. "Yes, Mother?"

"Maybe Gallium doesn't want to talk about that right now," she cautioned.

She set the packages down and placed a hand on her hip. "Well, why not? He's a war hero. Every Coldarian except for Lady Alarah is singing his praises." She looked over at him. "You should hold your head up high. Your win on Platirius is a win for all of us Coldarians. You've made us all very proud, Gallium."

Unable to think of a proper response, he nodded at her.

Etienne clapped her hands. "Well, let me take your dishes to the dining chamber. Then, we can sit and have refreshments until the other guests arrive. All of our daughters and their families are joining us, so we've prepared quite a spread."

It was true. There were dainty cheese balls, mutton meatballs swimming in a thick, sweet sauce, mushroom caps stuffed with crab and shrimp, creamy cheese soup, fried quail, sea scallops, baked trout, sea bass, braised beef, duck breasts in a spicy, citrus glaze, fried cabbage with sausages, and smothered pork and onions.

Dr. Barrios's favorite chicken cylinders in herbed bread crumbs sat beside potato pancakes, creamed potatoes, honeyed sweet potatoes, smoked corn, green beans with almonds and bits of ham, creamed spinach, candied fruit and nuts, chicken stew, beef stew, and six kinds of bread.

The ChildForms were excited to see tall chocolate cakes, coconut cakes, lemon, peach, and blueberry pies, apple fritters, and sticky glazed doughnuts. Mrs. Guilde proudly added a half-dozen of her decadent cheese pies to the loaded dessert tables.

Etienne sank into the plushness of the settee. "I've been cooking for days. I don't want to see a crumb left behind."

"Oh, I don't think there will be," said Mrs. Guilde. "You have a huge family. Had my Harold lived, Legend would've had lots of brothers and sisters running about."

The TeleShield's scanner buzzed again. King Carlomon strode into the cottage, his arms laden with gifts. His eyes twinkled with merriment. "Do you have room for three more?"

Before anyone could answer, Queen Dellah stepped around him, holding Princess Vivant's hand. "Hello, everyone! I've been waiting for this feast all year. King Dubian sends his apologies, but he's not able to join us. Since he's temporarily in charge of the military, someone had to stay behind to make sure Platirius is protected."

That was only half of the truth. Viewing the celebration period as a perfect time to place distance between them, she hadn't given him a choice in joining her and their daughter.

He wasn't happy to stay behind, but she didn't care. Judging from their smiles, she knew they were silently thanking The One for his absence. So was she.

Etienne hurried to embrace her. "Oh, Queen Dellah! We're so happy to see you! Amos, please grab the overstuffed chair in the library and bring it for her?" She turned to her and bowed. "We're so honored you've joined us."

She smiled at her. "No need for formalities, Etienne. I'm home now and we're surrounded by family. I intend to enjoy myself and eat like a glutton." She sniffed the air. "It appears you've outshone all the staff in the royal dining chamber this year. I expected nothing less from you."

Gallium and Dr. Barrios helped Amos place three large chairs in front of the fireplace. Grateful to be off her feet, she sat down. "Princess Vivant, where are your manners? Say hello to everyone."

"Hello," said Princess Vivant shyly. Everyone greeted her and noted that she was growing up to be as stunning as Queen Dellah. She took a seat next to her mother and looked around at the beautifully decorated social chamber.

Amos gestured for King Carlomon to sit with them as Etienne handed them steaming cups of tea. "Princess Vivant, I believe there's a nice selection of cookies for you to try," said Etienne.

The princess's eyes lit up. Eagerly, she looked at her mother.

"Just a couple of cookies," she warned. "You don't want to ruin your supper. It smells like Etienne has prepared a fine banquet for us."

King Carlomon raised his cup to Gallium. "I can't thank you enough for defeating those nasty Kikhanians, Gallium. You've earned your appointment to general. I think it's been a long time coming."

"Yes, he certainly did," said Queen Dellah. "Queen Amori and I have always been friends, even before she married King Hitam. I wish she had chosen a better husband."

She tugged softly on Princess Vivant's braid. "It's difficult to think clearly when you're in love," she said sadly. "I hate to think how the war is affecting her since she just gave birth a short while ago. As for her husband, I have no sympathy. He should've known better to attack us."

Amos and Etienne looked at each other and smiled. "We have a general in the family," said Amos proudly.

As more guests poured in and praised Gallium, his anxiety significantly decreased. They didn't fear him or treat him any differently. He silently thanked The One for bestowing compassion and understanding on them.

Etienne squeezed Amos's hand. "All of our friends, ChildForms, and grand ChildForms are under one roof tonight. We are so blessed and thankful to our Savior for being merciful to us."

Throughout the evening, they sang songs by the fire and exchanged gifts. Gallium blushed when he opened Legend's gift.

She saucily nibbled on a cookie. "I worry about you getting cold at night in the military chamber. So I decided to knit some warm underclothing for you."

"I—er, thank you, Legend. I'll be sure to wear them."

Everyone admired the diamond and sapphire necklace and bracelet ensemble he gave her—especially Legend. "I've never had anything this fine in my lifespan." Clutching the set to her chest, her eyes filled with tears. "Thank you so much. I'll always cherish them."

"There's more," said Gallium. The deep timbre in his voice caught her attention. He stood up and pulled her to her feet. Getting down on one knee, he produced an expensive-looking box. She gasped when he opened it, revealing a colossal diamond ring.

"Legend, I've never been in love before until you, and I'll never love anyone after you. Will you please be my wife?"

For one who seldom held her tongue, his proposal had rendered her speechless. Quickly, she wiped away the tears flooding down her cheeks.

"Gallium, you've done the impossible," teased Mrs. Guilde. "I've never seen Legend so quiet."

Everyone laughed, including Legend.

"Hey," he said. "You aren't going to leave me on my knees forever, are you? Help me out here!"

"Of course I'll marry you. You're the most amazing and wonderful MaleForm I've ever met. I love you so much."

He stood and clutched her tightly to his muscular chest. Lost in celebrating the newly engaged couple, no one realized a WomanForm was gazing through the window at them. She fled with tears streaming down her face before they saw her.

"Well, Etienne and Mrs. Guilde, it looks like another spectacular wedding awaits us in the future," said Queen Dellah.

Mrs. Guilde dried her eyes. "I can't wait to see how beautiful Legend will look in her gown."

Queen Dellah accepted a cookie from Princess Vivant. "My best seamstress will make it," she said. "Legend, you'll be the wife of a general. I hope you won't think I'm overstepping, but I intend for every jaw to drop when they see you—including General Barrios."

Gallium wiped Legend's tears. "Of course not. That's so kind of you, Queen Dellah," she said.

Queen Dellah looked at her father. "Our plan was for all Coldarians to live prosperously and it's succeeded. This is only the beginning for us."

Everyone raised their glasses in salute. Over the next few days, they laughed and enjoyed each other's company. By the end of the week, none of them wanted the celebration to end. Reluctantly, they said their goodbyes, promising to rejoin the following year to celebrate their good fortunes.

King Dubian was sitting in the den when Queen Dellah and Princess Vivant arrived.

She peered into the darkness and turned on all the lights. "Why are you sitting here alone in the dark?" she asked.

Surprised, he looked up at them and smiled. "Ah! My darlings are finally home!" Princess Vivant ran into his outstretched arms. "Did you have fun?"

"Oh, Father! We had cookies and cake and all sorts of good things to eat! And Grandfather ate so much, his belly poked out!"

He chuckled ruefully. He'd hoped Queen Dellah would invite him to the celebration, but she had chosen to go without him. "Now that's funny! It's a compliment to the cook to eat well."

His eyes met his wife's. The distance between them had grown wider than Platirius and Jupiter. He was at a loss for how to make things right. Hiding his melancholy under the elation he didn't feel, he smiled at her. "And you? Did you and the little one take it easy and eat vegetables and fruit as Dr. Krause suggested?"

She shrugged one shoulder. "Only if they were drowning in cream and butter."

"Dellah!"

She waved a hand at him. "Oh, don't start nagging me, Dubian. JehovRi comes once a year. It was nice to honor The One's LifeCelebration and welcome the new year on Coldarius. I've missed it so much."

"Well then, how do you feel about bringing your family here to live with us? King Carlomon is getting older, and you have a sister, right? Opal?"

She stared at him. "How did you know about Opal? She's been living on Earth for many years."

He stood and rubbed her shoulders. "I don't know much about her—just her name. I don't even know what she looks like."

Her mouth opened, then closed. What he didn't know wouldn't hurt him.

"But if it makes you happy, I'd like to bring them here so you won't be so lonely when I'm away."

"I don't think Father would want to leave Coldarius, and I'm pretty sure Opal wants to remain on Earth. She's built a life there as a spy for us. I'd love it if Father were closer, but he has a kingdom to run."

He kept his smile in place. "Well, your mother has a few family members left. We have plenty of room if they want to join us."

He pointed to an open space of land. "I could have new chambers built for them in the blink of a star. Allow me to speak with your father, please? If he won't come, maybe he'll give his permission for the others to live here. I really think it would be a good move for our family."

Feeling overwhelmed, she nodded. "I'm tired. Please alert a NurseForm to get our daughter ready for bed."

"Of course. You go up and I'll join you in a moment. In a while, My Queen."

He hadn't missed the surprise on her lovely face. He'd never wanted to share her with anyone—including King Carlomon. Now he wanted to bring her extended family to the palace.

What on Platirius has gotten into him?

"In a while, Dubian," she said, giving him a quick peck on the cheek.

He stood, watching her leave with his hand resting on his cheek. The smoldering lust in his eyes made the NurseForm's stomach queasy. He hadn't noticed when she arrived or when she silently took the princess's hand and led her away. He stared down the hall long after the queen was no longer in sight.

Shrieking alarms sounded throughout the palace. There was chaos everywhere as Beings hurried in and out the doors. King Dubian had dispatched Dr. Krause to his bed chamber.

Queen Dellah and the new InfantForm were in distress. She lay on the floor, crying out in anguish.

He firmly held a pillow to her vulva to staunch the flow of blood, cursing as it gushed out and onto his hands. Blood pooled from underneath her night robe, spilling onto the platinum floors.

"Where is Dr. Krause? GET HER IN HERE!" he shouted.

The medical staff rushed in and lifted the queen on a stretcher. Frantically, he grabbed Dr. Krause by the collar. "You said bed rest would help her! Now look at her! If my wife dies, YOU die. Do you understand?" he shouted.

"Yes, King Dubian! We'll do everything to save her."

"Save her first!" he ordered. "As for the InfantForm...if it dies, then it dies. I want my wife to live!"

Dr. Krause nodded and struggled out of his iron grip. "Let's get her to the medical chamber now!" she said.

Gallium and the rest of the soldiers joined the crowd surrounding the medical chamber to wait for news about her.

"King Dubian won't allow me to assist Dr. Krause," said Dr. Barrios. "I have more training and experience than she does! I should be in there!"

Gallium swiftly pivoted toward him. "Why won't he let you help her?"

"He doesn't want me to see her unclothed form," muttered Dr. Barrios.

"But that's ridiculous," said Dora Reese. "You're a physician! You're not a wayward pervert like him!"

"Watch your mouth, Dora Reese," warned Sandi Childler. "Remember the queen's decree. You're right, of course, but we're not allowed to say anything against a royal."

Dora smacked her teeth. "Who is here to enforce it on the mooncalf's behalf? He's rolling the dice on her life! I don't want her to die."

Gallium placed a hand on her shoulder. "We all know what you mean, Dora. Trust me, we feel the same."

Major Kron came running up to them. "What's wrong with Queen Dellah?" Everyone ignored him.

"Watch your words in front of him," Gallium whispered to Dora. She gave Major Kron a scathing glance and turned away.

General Iham also joined them. "I just heard about Queen Dellah. We have to warn King Dubian! General Sodom was just killed on Kikhani. Our soldiers are without a leader. Someone has to take his place and fast."

"He's in the medical chamber with Queen Dellah," said Gallium. "He's in no position to make that call now."

"Well, someone has to go!" cried General Iham. "I'd go, but Queen Dellah ordered me to stay here. We can't leave them out there on their own."

"We won't," said Gallium. He turned to look at Major Kron. "You're up, Major Kron! Prepare to go to Kikhani."

All eyes swung from Gallium to the young Major. He couldn't disobey his order—Gallium outranked him.

Major Kron saluted him and General Iham. "I'll need a thousand soldiers to go with me. I can dispatch another two from Maieman."

General Iham nodded. "Take them, son. Just be sure to end King Hitam and return safely. This war has gone on long enough. The queen shouldn't have to deal with this and what she's going through. If you take Kikhani, it's a guaranteed promotion to general."

"Shouldn't we tell the king?" asked Major Kron.

"King Dubian's focus is on his wife," said Gallium. "Do you really think he'll leave her side to listen to what you have to say? He doesn't care what happens to you."

None of you do. But I'll show you, thought Major Kron. "I'll be off then," he said. "May The One bless Queen Dellah with long life."

"Good riddance," said Corporal Canob when he was out of earshot.

General Iham looked at Gallium. "He has an impressive record, but he's young. He may die over there, then you or I will have to go to Kikhani."

"He's too arrogant to die," said Gallium. "He'll get the job done. If he doesn't, I'll go and end it all for good. Right now, we need to pray for our queen."

General Ihan nodded. "I've sent word to her father. He's on his way here."

Gallium blew on his hands to warm them. "Good. Now we'll just have to wait and see what happens. She's strong. I know she'll make it. She has to."

A dark cloud descended over the medical chamber as the Coldarians and Platirians joined hands and prayed for their queen. After an hour passed, King Carlomon arrived.

Quickly jumping off his horse, he rushed over to Gallium and General Iham. "Where's my daughter?"

"She's inside the medical chamber, King Carlomon," said a NurseForm running down the stairs. "I've been waiting to take you to her."

He ran as fast as his leg would allow. His breathing slowed as he reached Queen Dellah, who lay still on the bed. He picked up her freezing hand and warmed it between his.

"Dellah," he said miserably. "I'm here. I've come to take care of you."

Her eyes fluttered open. "Father," she whispered. "Did you see my baby? She's beautiful."

Another NurseForm brought the healthy baby to him. He peered into her small face and smiled. His daughter was right. His granddaughter was absolutely breathtaking. She had a mass of curly black hair, silver eyes, and deep dimples. He gently kissed her soft cheek.

"I see her, Dellah," said King Carlomon. "She's positively perfect! She looks exactly as you did when you were born."

King Dubian sat motionless, clutching her other hand as if he were afraid to let go. He barely glanced at the InfantForm.

"Please bring her to me," she ordered in a weak voice. "Lay her on my chest." She looked down at her baby, gently stroking her hair. "Her name," she said, struggling to speak, "is Princess Revari Ava Amorous."

"We can deal with that later, My Queen. Right now, our top priority is getting you better," said King Dubian.

Her fist clenched tightly. "Your priorities should lie with our daughter!" she snapped. The monitors above her head began sounding off.

"Alright now!" said King Carlomon. "Dellah, please calm yourself!" He turned to King Dubian. "Will you be quiet? You're making things worse by upsetting her!"

King Dubian's lip quivered. "Forgive me, Dellah. I don't mean to make you angry."

"Maybe you should leave," said King Carlomon.

He looked up at him in shock. "What? No! I'm not leaving my wife. She needs me!"

"What she needs," said King Carlomon through clenched teeth, "is peace of mind. You don't seem to know how to give it to her."

He glared at him. "I'm not leaving her—"

"Yes, you will," said Queen Dellah. She held Princess Revari close to her breasts. "You haven't changed—you're still selfish and cruel. And...you don't want our baby. I know you don't, Dubian!" She began to cry softly.

"That's not true, Dellah!"

King Carlomon advanced around the bed. "Get out or I'll throw you out," he snapped. "I never should've allowed you to marry my daughter."

"Just leave, Dubian. Now," she said. "You being here is too much for me to handle."

He rested his hand on her thigh. "All right, I'll go, but I'm coming back as soon as you're calm. I love you, Dellah. I refuse to lose you."

He gave King Carlomon a scathing glance before he exited in a huff.

She stroked the thick mass of curls on the baby's head. "Father, please hold her?"

"Of course," he said, taking up the small, soft bundle. He smiled down into her tiny face. "She's a healthy one, isn't she? She'll be a good eater."

She smiled, then grimaced. "Yes, I have a feeling she will, but I'm too weak to nurse her."

"We have milk prepared for the new princess, Your Highness," said a NurseForm. "With your permission, she can be fed now."

"Please let my father feed her," she said. She rolled her head on the pillow. The pain hadn't stopped since the baby was born. She had slipped in and out of consciousness for hours. "Send for Princess Vivant and have Gallium come to see me."

The NurseForm bowed. "Yes, Queen Dellah."

She ran to retrieve Gallium while King Carlomon sat down to feed Princess Revari.

Princess Vivant arrived first. Worry stretched across her face as she stared at her mother's ashen face. Her skin felt cool to the touch. "Mother, it's me. Open your eyes. Are you sick?"

She squeezed her little hand. "I'm fine, Darling. I just wanted you to see your baby sister."

Princess Vivant looked at Princess Revari, who waved a tiny fist in the air. "She's so beautiful! She looks just like a doll!" She planted a soft kiss on her plump cheek. "I can't wait to play with her."

"That won't be for a while, Dear. You have to give her time to grow a bit."

"Yes, Mother. Wow! She looks just like me!" she said happily.

Not wanting to alarm her, she struggled to keep her eyes open. At times, it felt as if she were floating out of her body toward the roof of the medical chamber. She nodded to a NurseForm to take Princess Vivant away.

"But, Mother, why can't I stay with you and the new baby?"

She stroked her soft hair. She didn't want to leave her daughters. Silently, she bargained with The One to allow her to stay with them. "I need to rest now. Come and give Mother a kiss. I'll see you in a while."

Princess Vivant's eyes filled with tears. She kissed her mother's cheek and kissed Princess Revari again. King Carlomon embraced her before laying the baby in the small, elaborately decorated bed. Gently, he pushed it next to his daughter's bed and leaned down to kiss her on the forehead.

"I hear Gallium coming. I'll be back when you've rested up a bit," he promised.

She grabbed his hand and held it to her face. "No, sit in the chair next to me. There's no need to leave. I'll be fine, Father. Please don't worry about me."

He held onto her hand. "You're my daughter. It's my job to worry about you." An image of King Dubian flashed in his mind. He shook his head in disgust. "Someone has to."

Gallium bowed to King Carlomon before hurrying to Queen Dellah's bedside. Smiling down at the little princess, he grabbed the queen's hand when she reached for him.

"How are you feeling, Queen Dellah?"

She squeezed his hand. "I'm not going to make it, Gallium."

"Oh, come on! Don't talk like that!"

"Shh, listen to me. I've lost too much blood. No one has my blood type." She winced. The pain was getting worse. "It'll take too long for Princess Opal to arrive. Listen to what I'm going to tell you." Her eyes filled with tears. "Gallium, please promise me something?"

He tightened his grip on her dainty hand. "I'll promise you anything you want if you fight to stay alive, My Queen."

"You must protect Princess Revari. Please—please don't let Dubian hurt my baby!"

"Please don't cry. You know I won't allow anything to happen to Princess Revari or Princess Vivant."

"He won't blame Vivant. It's Revari he'll despise. He never wanted her."

If he ever thought there was reason to call King Dubian an idiot, the time was now. Who wouldn't want a baby as lovely as Princess Revari?

"If I go, he'll blame my baby. He's so twisted and self-hating. I should've known King Anemi and Queen Zherta had damaged his mind beyond repair, but I didn't! I never should've married him. I thought I was doing the right thing for Coldarius, but I regret bearing his ChildForms. There's too much evil inside him."

Her wide eyes flew to his. "Promise me you'll stay by Princess Revari's side for the rest of her lifespan. Never leave her, Gallium. Promise me!"

"I promise I'll protect her until the day I die. You have my word on that. I know King Dubian is crazy. We all know it. I won't allow his madness to affect her, but you need to stay and fight for her too. And Princess Vivant—your father—your sister—all of us. We need you."

"I've set things in place for your protection too. He'll never be able to harm you or any Coldarian."

He rubbed her hand in both of his. It felt like ice. "If he does, I want him dead. If he hurts any of my Beings, promise me you'll end him."

Feeling tears rolling down his face, hot and fast, he nodded. "I'll do anything you ask, My Queen. But let's not focus on that right now. Okay?"

She held tightly to his hand. "You've been a good friend to me. I'll never forget you, Gallium. I'm going to miss you so much!"

"Don't say that! You're going to survive. You have no idea how many Beings are out there praying for you. Don't give up now!"

Dr. Krause hurried to her bedside. "Queen Dellah, we'll give you a serum to clot the bleeding. We're still waiting on word from Princess Opal. Do you want me to find King Dubian?"

"No! By The One, I don't want his face to be the last I see." She beamed up at Gallium. "The view I have before I see The One is the best a queen could have." She reached up and cupped his bearded cheek. "In a while, General Barrios," she whispered.

She shuddered and looked up into Space. King Carlomon held tightly to her hand as Gallium watched the light drift slowly from her eyes.

His chest heaved as he sobbed uncontrollably. "In a while...My Queen."

The death bells sounded across the grounds of the palace. Shock reverberated through the crowd as her loyal subjects lamented over their loss.

The queen of Platirius was dead.

King Dubian rushed into the medical chamber. "Who gave the order to sound death bells? Have you all gone mad?"

He ran to her side. "Noooo! Noooo! She's not gone!" He screamed and began throwing things around the medical chamber. "Noooooo! It isn't possible!"

He grabbed Dr. Krause by the throat. "Why didn't you call for me? Why did you let her die without me?" Her eyes bulged as he proceeded to squeeze harder. "Are you not a doctor? Why didn't you save my wife?"

King Carlomon and Gallium grabbed him, trying to free her from his grip. "King Dubian! Have you lost your senses?" shouted King Carlomon. "Let her go!"

But he held onto her, trying to choke the life out of her.

"We need assistance in here!" shouted King Carlomon.

A group of soldiers rushed in to help pry the deranged king off the frightened physician.

"Take your filthy hands off me," he screamed.

"He's become unhinged," said King Carlomon. "Give him a sedative!"

The fury in King Dubian's eyes blazed over them. "No! You won't take me away from my wife! I'll kill you all! Do you hear me? You DIRTY Coldarians! I'll kill every last one of you!"

Gallium grabbed a syringe from a bewildered NurseForm and stuck it into his neck. He shouted as the sedative was pumped into his vein. When he finally stopped struggling, Gallium tossed him to the floor like a sack of potatoes.

Panting heavily, Gallium looked over at Queen Dellah, then down at him. "To think he carried on like this in front of her. He has no respect for anyone!" He turned to the soldiers. "Drag him to his bed chamber and lock him up. Don't let him come out until I give the order. He's too crazy to roam about."

"Yes, General Barrios!" It took four of them to lift him off the floor.

"I said drag, not carry him. He weighs more than a horse. Make it easy on yourselves."

They threw him to the ground and dragged him up the palace stairs.

King Carlomon looked from Gallium to his daughter. "By The One, what will we do now? He's in no position to care for my granddaughters. When I think back on it, all the warning signs were there. When I met with him to finalize the merger, I sensed something was wrong. I never should've ignored my instincts."

Gallium perused Queen Dellah's motionless form. "None of this is your fault. He's responsible for his own actions. I promised her I wouldn't allow him to hurt them. I intend to keep that promise, My King."

King Carlomon pulled the silk sheet up to her chin. He couldn't bear to cover her face. "I wish she had married you. Maybe she'd still be alive."

Gallium looked up at the window of King Dubian's bed chamber, but saw no sign of him. "I think if we had known this would happen, we all would've made different choices, but what's done is done. It'll be difficult, but for the sake of the princesses, we have to follow her wishes. We can't allow that imbecile to destroy everything she's built."

Outside the medical chamber, the Coldarians and Platirians wept for their queen. The death bells continued to ring loudly into the night. They looked up into Space and spied a craft bearing the crest of the kingdom of Coldarius landing in the middle of the palace's grounds.

A WomanForm descended from the craft's stairs. As she drew closer, wailing and shocked gasps surrounded her. Slowly, she removed the hood from her head. Her silver eyes assessed each of their faces.

"I am Princess Opal of Coldarius," she said. "Please take me to my sister, Queen Dellah."

Epilogue

The voices had hounded him relentlessly since they locked him away in darkness. He tried to beat down the heavy door, but it wouldn't yield. *What are they doing to her?* he wondered. King Anemi stepped out of the shadows. He spun around to face the silent figure.

"Father! They're trying to take my wife away from me!"

That's because you're weak, Dubian. You were never right for her. Now they're going to take Princess Vivant and return to Coldarius. The new InfantForm belongs to Gallium, not you. She was never yours. You murdered my son to have her only for her to leave you after she's stripped Platirius down to nothing!

King Dubian shook his head. "No, you're wrong! You don't know her! I've been a better husband to her than my brother would've been!"

King Anemi's chilling eyes looked through him. *I know she laid with a commoner in your bed and bore his seed. And I know you aren't the rightful king of Platirius. Her father will kill you, Dubian. Then he'll absorb Platirius into Coldarius. You've ruined everything I've built! I curse the day I learned your mother was carrying you. I should've had her beheaded and you gutted from her treacherous womb*! A long, bony finger pointed at King Dubian. *Platirius will fall because of you.*

He grinned. "No. I will be the greatest king to sit on the throne. King Carlomon will never take Platirius or Queen Dellah away from me. You'll see, Father."

As King Anemi faded away, King Dubian ran to the window and stared down at the Beings still gathered outside the medical chamber.

"All of you will see," he promised. "I'll destroy Gallium and Coldarius. I swear by The One, anyone who opposes me will die!"

As the death bells sounded throughout the darkness of Space, Princess Revari began to cry.

Coldarius: The Betrayal Book II

K ing Micah gathered everyone inside the worship chamber to witness the promotion. Major Kron had expected the Platirians not to support him. To his surprise, they'd grown weary of King Dubian's madness. Loud cheers rang out as Major Kron became General Kron of Platirius.

He stood at the podium with pride shining in his eyes. "Thank you all for sharing this prestigious honor with me. We all know Platirius is one of the greatest empires in the galaxy. Since I was a ChildForm, I've heard of the epic battles fought and won by the former kings. To let its glory end would be a disgrace. I intend to bring respect and prosperity back to it!"

The halls thundered with roars of support for their new leader. But he hadn't won over everyone. More than a few of King Dubian's supporters subtly murmured their displeasure.

"When will King Dubian be released from the Chamber of Despair?" asked Chief Counselor Garoni.

Silence descended over the crowd when the oldest member of the justice council approached the podium.

"Never in Platirius's history has a king been locked away in his own mental chamber. He's been unjustly imprisoned—without even a trial. Would you say that's fair to him, General Kron? After all, he's the son of King Anemi, not you." He nodded toward King Micah. "What gives your father the right to take away his power and hand it to you?"

An uneasiness shifted among the MaleForms. Chief Counselor Garoni focused his attention on them. "The throne has always passed within the bloodlines. King Dubian is a second-born son, but he's still royalty. How are we comfortable with watching an outsider steal it for himself?"

"That's not what my son is trying to do," said King Micah.

The Chief Counselor's eyes narrowed. "That's exactly what he's trying to do," he said coldly. "He hasn't been on Platirius for a year, and isn't old enough to shave, yet you believe he should take charge of our planet? If you want him to govern a kingdom, then speed up your death and have him take your place on Maieman. We won't sit by and watch this treasonous act bear fruit."

General Kron could feel his support dwindling under the weight of the Chief Counselor's influence. He placed his hand on King Micah's arm to prevent him from attacking the elder Justice Counselor.

Chief Counselor Garoni's eyes, as black as ravens, glared balefully at him. "What do you say, General Kron? Shall we bring you before the justice council to convince us this isn't treason?

I'll warn you, if you lose your case, you'll be thrown into the Flames of Justice."

He smirked at King Micah before shifting his steely gaze to the young general. "Of course, that could be avoided if King Dubian were released today. Then we can all get back to normal."

D.L.'s Note

C ongratulations, Dear Reader!

You've just ended your first journey into the world of Coldarius! My new fantasy world was born when a pivotal scene in *Platirius: The Rise of Reve Book II,* held my attention long after I'd written it. The exchange between Gallium and General Lyric was explosive! His quick wit and sharp tongue motivated me to give him a backstory.

In addition, I felt Coldarius deserved more than an honorable mention in the Platirius series. King Dubian had such a strong presence, his spirit hovered heavily between the stories. I felt it was necessary to show where the queens acquired their strength and bravery—their mother. And so, Queen Dellah was born.

What a formidable female character! Planning her death was so sad, I literally cried when I wrote it and every time I had to edit the story. I felt her loss just as if I were a character who had walked beside her. If I conveyed that level of emotion to you, then I've done my job.

I was happy to have the chance to continue developing the sultry and ambitious General Legend too. My goal was to bring most of the characters to life that weren't too heavy on the side of good or evil. Each one has different shades of color that make them relatable, even though they live in a fantasy world.

I love all the characters in the Coldarius series. I hope you will too. Stick with me for one more ride around planet Coldarius. A brand new character is coming that will shake things up!

Until next time, dear Readers!

D.L. xoxo

Author's Bio

D.L. Hannah was born in Youngstown, Ohio. She is a writer, entrepreneur, and host of the Amerisogyny podcast. She is a Psi Chi and Alpha Kappa Delta member and earned a Bachelor of Arts degree in Clinical-Community Psychology from Walsh University. For over twenty years, she has been a strong advocate for children diagnosed with autism. She now lives in North Carolina with her family.

Join My VIP List

Sign up for my VIP List @www.dlhannah.com

Also by D.L. Hannah